How Much the
Heart Can Hold

How Much the Heart Can Hold

Seven Stories on Love

Carys Bray

Rowan Hisayo Buchanan

Bernardine Evaristo

Grace McCleen

Donal Ryan

Nikesh Shukla

D.W. Wilson

SCEPTRE

First published in Great Britain in 2016 by Sceptre
An imprint of Hodder & Stoughton
An Hachette UK company

First published in paperback in 2017

1

A CIP catalogue record for this title is available from the British Library

ISBN 978 1 473 64945 3

Typeset in Sabon by Palimpsest Book Production Limited,
Falkirk, Stirlingshire

Printed and bound by Clays Ltd, St Ives plc

Hodder & Stoughton policy is to use papers that are natural, renewable
and recyclable products and made from wood grown in sustainable forests.
The logging and manufacturing processes are expected to conform to the
environmental regulations of the country of origin.

Hodder & Stoughton Ltd
Carmelite House
50 Victoria Embankment
London EC4Y 0DZ

www.hodder.co.uk

Contents

Introduction

Each person I've told about this book has had a similar reaction: a polite smile, a head tilt and a noise ('ahhh' or 'oooh', sometimes, 'mmmm'). Because they are, of course, assuming that this is another collection of stories about romantic love. They're expecting candles and chocolates, roses and star-crossed lovers; stolen kisses, maybe, and acts of fate. I can't say that I blame them. The word 'love' comes loaded with centuries of discourse, which for the most part has focussed on a binary (lover/beloved), romantic concept.

But look further back and you'll find that the Ancient Greeks, especially, had different words for love, referring to a different aspect of the idea: from storge (familial love), to agape (charitable, expansive love); philautia (love of the self), and eros (sexual passion and desire). I felt that these different types of love were ripe for exploration, and what better medium than that which bucks all attempts to make it conform: the short story.

When I approached the seven, brilliant, authors of the stories within, I gave them a choice of different types of love, along with a vague line on what each one meant (incidentally, I should note here that I am no expert on Ancient Greek, so any mistakes regarding the types of love are entirely my own. I hope you can forgive an overenthusiastic fiction editor and her dictionary all errors). Other than that, I didn't give a steer on what the story should address, or how the love they'd chosen should be represented. When all the stories came back, the thing that struck me most – the uniting feature of each tale – was that the love they chose was always characterised by action, and resulted in transformation. Love in these stories is rarely static, but constantly changing and developing. It is, universally, an active force.

After reading the stories, as I had hoped, I thought more about love as a plural concept; but more than this, I was led to think about love as a tool for change. I hope that these seven wonderful stories will leave you with the same conviction.

Emma Herdman, Sceptre
Summer 2016

La Douleur Exquise

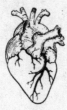

From French

douleur – pain; exquise – exquisite

Exquisite pain of unrequited love; feeling, not a state.

La Douleur Exquise is a French term for which there is no direct English translation. Whilst it is sometimes construed simply as unrequited love, it is instead the (exquisite) *feeling* of your love not being reciprocated, rather than an objective description of a relationship between two people. It describes the ache, specifically of the one whose love is unrequited, associated with a love that is unattainable whether through circumstance or choice.

Before It Disappears

Rowan Hisayo Buchanan

Richard swirls shampoo into Joy's scalp. His hands emerge netted in hair. It has only just grown back and is already coming out. Ever since leaving the hospital, she has returned to her strictures of starvation. He wonders if she remembers their honeymoon five years ago. They'd shared this same cottage, this same bath, and her hair had hung to her soft hips.

Naked, Joy's body seems like a mechanical device. It is something about the way her veins are wired in green and blue. Each pivot of her bones is visible. Richard runs the sponge over the grill of her ribs. He can't see her expression, but she doesn't pull away. For the moment she is allowing him to do this small thing for her.

Steam pours up from the hot water. The air is thick with it. Richard begins to feel woozy. This excess of heat cannot be good for Joy. He stands, and undoes the latch on the small window. Outside, the rain mizzles and mumbles. Wind snatches the frame, pulling the window open. Too cold. Too hot. Where is just right?

The cottage in the Highlands is a last resort. He tries not to think of it as a hospice, but the hospital says the treatment isn't taking. Her doctors have shrugged and abdicated from the loop of remission and relapse.

'Do you remember when I lifted you over the threshold?' He is speaking to the top of her head. She does not look up. They married at twenty-four, the first of their friends. He would not have guessed that at thirty-one he would have to carry her all the way from the car. 'And then you wanted to lift me? I didn't believe you could do it. But you did.' She'd wrapped herself around his knees and lifted his feet two inches from the ground, but *Remember*, he is trying to say, *remember you used to be strong.*

Richard leaves the window open, and sinks back down around his wife.

Joy leans backwards, tilting her face upwards and whispers; 'I saw a unicorn, on the roadside.'

Quips and fears tangle in Richard's throat. He knows that her refusal to eat is its own insanity, but he is not prepared for unicorns. The wind shifts and sweeps inside through the open window, wafting the steam back in. Pine needles pelt them. Gold and brown slivers. Evergreens are not always green it seems. She closes her eyes as pine-pins flick her face. Does she too feel them like tiny fingernails? They catch in her hair and float across the bathtub. One bobs against the freckle on her inside knee and others stick to the peaks of her hipbones. She twists her head, skin contorting around bone, and opens her mouth. In the centre of her tongue is one of the needles. She lisps, careful not to let her tongue curl, removing all the angles of her speech. Each *s* softened to a soupy *th*, each *r* to a digestible *w*.

'If I thwallow i- will I gwow a twee inthide o- me?'

Richard thinks that if she swallows it, it would be the first thing in forty-eight hours. He replies, 'A forest.'

Her mouth curves up as if to smile, but then swerves away from the expression. She spits the needle into the water. It hangs suspended in yellow saliva. Joy turns away. These past weeks, there have been many moments when she seemed on the cusp of forgetting her fury, but she always remembers.

Submerged in bathwater, Joy's feet look close to normal. The rippling liquid disguises the jagged bones. Under a regime of force-feeding, the nails have grown back short and pink. You could develop a fetish just from looking so long, but he has learned to take these tiny pleasures. He wonders if this is punishment for the fact that when he met her, he enjoyed how small she was, how she could be hoisted, rigged, lifted and dropped, how her body on his was an easy weight, how when they fucked, she seemed deliciously snappable. And now she is. The doctor said her bones were brittle. Lack of calcium was ageing her skeleton. As if impaired cardiac function and the risk of seizures were not enough, her very structure is failing. He presses his face against her neck, careful not to crush her. In the steam, he can't smell her, only the choke of lavender. If he doesn't fix this, he will lose even his wife's smell.

Richard carries her out of the bath and into bed. It is warm but he bundles Joy under two comforters. He likes to see her wrapped in this simulacrum of flesh. He sits on the edge of the bed until Joy's eyes slide shut. He reaches into his suitcase, where he had hidden a pot of honey and a brush inside a pair of white athletic socks. He moves slowly, tiptoeing back. Joy mumbles. Her face is so lovely in the half-light. He should be disgusted by her. At this stage of starvation, women aren't supposed to be beautiful. But she is exquisite.

His ex-girlfriend said he picked flawed women to distract himself from his own inadequacies – but ex-girlfriends always become psychologists. Still, it can't entirely be his fault could it?

Somewhere in there is a brain that has chosen to leave him gram by gram. She has to bear some responsibility. He doesn't want her to leave. He has never wanted that. He wants to shout. But he has shouted. Her mother has shouted in English and Shanghainese and a terrifying blend of the two, from which even Richard cowered. Shouting has not worked, and now it would only wake her.

The tiny jar of honey is stuck. His hand tenses. He bites his lip. The air bursts from his nostrils in stiff grunts. He forces himself to breathe silently. Finally the honey creaks open. He dips the brush inside. The golden meniscus resists, and then gives way. He eases the brush between her sunken lips. The face is stiff. The nostrils inflate. They are scabbed where the feeding tube used to go. The side of the nose is brown and clotted. He moves slowly, but carefully. He doesn't want to risk tickling her. The honey is a new idea and it was actually Joy who accidentally gave him the key. She wouldn't even taste the organic peaches that he'd bought from Waitrose. He'd put one in her favourite blue bowl, so the gold of the peach and the indigo glaze sang to one another. One of the things he's loved about her was how she'd cared about making each thing just right. But she'd refused to even put one slice of perfect peach on her tongue. Apparently, the mouth itself digests. Invisible enzymes pull sugars straight into the blood stream.

His brush becomes more confident. His movements speed. He strokes honey onto her lower lip, her gums, her teeth. It probably isn't good for her enamel but teeth only matter if you use them. The brush kisses her mouth again and again, and the last light of the day puddles in her honey-painted lips.

He wants her, but Joy is unfuckable. Her body cannot be jangled. It cannot be grasped. And even if it could, she is dry inside, or so he assumes. Hair loss there too, the curtains will soon match the carpet, both gone.

In the silent kitchen, Richard unbuckles his pants. Tomorrow, he will try again to save his wife. But he needs a moment to give in – to relax into desire. On his laptop, he pulls up Japanese comics. He has lost all his taste for videos, amateur or professional. Relishing the curve of fleshy thighs reminds him of what Joy doesn't have. So instead, he turns to these line drawings of women. They lack even colour.

Inky women never eat or drink. They weigh nothing at all. Tonight's girls have blank eyes. He thinks it signifies that pleasure has rolled their irises back in their heads. To Richard, they have the stare of Grecian statues: Blind Justice and her Sisters.

It isn't fair that even the porn is judging him. He made a mistake, yes, but cheating is normal. It is. Everyone cheats. Everyone.

He is a private client lawyer, he should know. His work is all prenuptials, trusts that give money without giving power, and of course wills. There's nothing like a last will and testament to show the dirty laundry. There are mistresses all over London, and little bastards in the most elite preparatory schools. It didn't even mean anything. It was just a drunk fuck with a colleague. How was he to know the woman who'd so eagerly lapped at his lips would feel the need to confess to her husband – a reckless moralist who decided Richard's wife *deserved to know*. And now, Joy is leaving him.

He would undo it if he could. He would. But the punishment is too vast. Illustrated semen spills over the inked lips of the girl, and all Richard can think of is hospital gruel pouring over Joy's mouth as he and the nurse beg and beg her to just swallow. The way it dripped down her neck. With a tissue, he wipes his tears first and then his dick.

He will fix this. Somehow.

Joy finds that time has gotten unreliable. It shows up and then vanishes. Long moments of white light. Conversations skip forwards like damaged cassettes. She expects that soon time will fall off the spool and tumble around her in long, brown ribbons. But what will that mean? She has no idea. She's cold. She's always cold. The air feels wet. This is a strange bed. Not the hospital bed. Slowly, she moves her hand to her face. Her face still hurts, but it is free. The tube is gone. It hurt, oh god it hurt, and as she thinks *hurt*, pain smashes her face. She shakes off the ghost tubes. Scotland, she is in Scotland. It smells of wet stone. It smells of old wood. There is a sticky sweetness in her mouth, but she does not trust her tongue any more.

Out the window, the pines cut the sky. Joy grew up in Canary Wharf and she thought the countryside would be mute. Instead, each noise is underlined by the quiet around it. A car on the road. Birds talking. Something heavy on gravel. Hooves.

She is sure they are hooves. She can't explain why she thinks this, but her heart clops.

Joy moves her head to the sound. The window is small. It has to be hooves, what else would beat out that steady clink? Outside is dark; she fumbles for the lamp. And then there is a reflected lamp hanging in the glass of the window. But then she sees it. The animal is right below the window. It takes her a moment to understand scale. It is too big to be a sheep, or a goat, the flanks too smooth. The head turns and it is yes, a horse. Pale ears, twitching, black eyes. But then the shape, long and pointed. The horn is grey as a chicken bone. Unicorn. She was wishing when she told Richard she'd seen a unicorn. It was only a white smudge in the trees that had made her think *unicorn*. This animal is so close that its flanks must be pressing against the side of the house. Maybe this is what happens when time falls off the loop. The creature is bigger than the Kia Richard hired.

For a minute, she thinks of calling out to her husband, as she once did when she saw something beautiful or alarming – a double-rainbow or a spider, or just a sale on the kind of juice he liked. But she doesn't do that now.

She woke up and it was all a dream, Joy had a teacher who failed you if you wrote that in one of your stories. She wondered what the teacher would have done if you'd written, *She woke up and it was all a dream and she remembered there was nothing worthwhile in this hamster wheel of life. That people would keep asking her what was so terrible and all she'd be able to say was all of this. All, all, all of this.*

She watches and tries to remember what she knows about unicorns. On her eleventh birthday, the glass unicorn arrived in the mail, addressed to her. Her father sent it. She'd asked for a new watch, the kind with a gummy strap that came in colours like cotton candy, marzipan and lemon drop. All the other girls had one. After unwrapping the unicorn, Joy refused to eat her cake. The unicorn was childish and stupid. How

8

old did her father think she was? Her mother, growing frustrated, shouted, 'If you don't want it, give it to your sister.'

An overdose of disappointment and fury had kept her awake all night. In the morning, she was allowed to stay home sick. Bored of daytime talk shows, she'd snuck into her sister's room. The unicorn stood at the head of a herd of plastic ponies. Joy held its flank up to her eye. The world viewed through the glassy haunches was blurred and beautiful, as the world is when seen through tears. She pressed the horn into the plush nub of her little finger. It was sharp as a spinning needle. The glass magnified the weft of her fingerprints. She pinched a hoof in her left hand, the body in her right. She let the smashability, crushability, powderability thrum between her fingers.

She let it live. Only once more did she think to smash it. Fifteen-year-old Joy was grounded for cutting. At night, her mum locked the kitchen knives in her own bedroom. During the day, the knives were kept in her handbag. Joy slipped into her sister's room – broken glass works as well as any knife. But her sister was also a teenager and the horses had joined the Salvation Army. The shelf was a galaxy of plastic earrings.

Joy blinks and the unicorn is gone. Richard is snoring next to her. The green clock glows five a.m. Sleep smothers her mind again.

The next day the rain has ended. August is back on, at least for now. Richard takes her to a castle. There are lots around here. On their honeymoon, they visited the most impressive and to Richard it just looked like a big house warted with turrets. This second time, even in the bee-confettied summer air, it still looks like that.

Last time, Joy had liked the castle. They'd taken their picture with this guy who had bagpipes.

Richard pushes Joy's wheelchair into the cafeteria. 'Two teas with milk please. And a shortbread. Do you take cards?'

The wheelchair pings as he bumps metal chair legs. 'Excuse me, excuse me.'

He removes the honey jar from his bag. In the light, he sees that at the mouth of the glass, sugar diamonds have formed. The spoon scrapes them away as he plunges it in for the golden honey. Then he spins the spoon in her tea, careful not to hit the sides of the china. He wants even the sound of the tea to soothe.

'Just a sip, Joy. Just a sip. You love honey. We bought this together, at the farmers' market. You remember. You said it was the best sort. It's organic.'

Perhaps he should have seen this coming. But he didn't. This was supposed to be over before they ever met. The couples' therapist said that fault was not a useful construct – the doling out of guilt and blame would hurt them both. But he'd known. He'd known from the beginning. Early on, Joy told him that she once struggled with an eating disorder. It seemed sweet then. They were lying in bed together her forehead pressing against his, her lips confessing the secrets of her teenage-life right into the cavity of his mouth as if he would swallow them.

So was it his fault for not predicting this? Or hers for implying it was over? Or his for fucking that girl? Or Joy's for overreacting? Or his for not being able to put this back together? Or?

'No. Not thirsty.' Joy shakes her head.

'You can't do this to me,' he says. 'Please.'

Her hands sit still on her lap like they are already dead. He eats the shortbread, barely feeling it in his throat. Summer light catches on the fine hairs that now grow on her arms. His mother was upset that he was dating a Chinese girl, but now Joy doesn't look Chinese so much as alien. How is it that he still thinks she's beautiful? But he does. That other girl, she was just a break, a slip up.

'I'm sorry. I'm sorry. Sorry,' he says. His dad used to say *Sorry means you won't do it again*. And he won't. He has said it so many times that now all he hears is Sorrow. I am sorrow. Sorrow. Blunt-toothed sorrow that is grinding them both down. 'Why Joy?' he asks. 'Why?' Another word he has said too many times. Joy shrugs. He has raised his voice. At the next table, the French tourists are looking over. He doesn't know how to say fuck off and mind your own business in French. He hasn't studied the language since he was fifteen and even then he could barely order a croissant. But of course, he is a spectacle. He is yelling at a wheelchair-bound woman. Even when he's trying to fix this, somehow he's the bastard.

'I didn't mean to. I mean obviously. But you were just. I was just. It was tiring you know. All the time.' Joy had always looked at him with eyes that were a little too wide, as if he had all the answers. He went out and took on the world for her, and she loved him. That was the deal. She clung to his hand at night. When she listened to his day at work, she really listened, the muscles under her eyes flexing with each victory and defeat. If he got a paper cut, Joy's hand hurt. And yet it had been good to feel that other girl's teeth crash against his mouth, her body trip and clang against his to ugly fuck. It was wrong. He'd known it was wrong. But he'd been so, so tired of being the hero. He hadn't realised that being the villain would be just as crushing.

'You can't leave me.'

She doesn't even bother looking up. Is it a lack of muscular or emotional strength that keeps her from meeting his eye?

'You know you aren't fat. This is ridiculous. You're too intelligent for this.' He has said all of these things before.

Joy is aware that Richard is telling her she isn't fat. At the hospital, people kept telling her she wasn't fat. The problem is more complicated than that. All flesh disgusts her. The way it peels and flakes. The way if you cut it, it scabs in amber creases. The very fleshness of it. She feels about her flesh the way that other people feel about vomit. A bucket of sick might be worse than a teaspoon of it, but how would you feel if you were stuck carrying a spoon of vomit everywhere? And food too. Looking at the way grease rises on steak makes her think of nothing more than sweaty buttocks. Even vegetables are veined and gross with life.

Richard is drinking his tea. Each time he pours, the pot drools brown liquid onto the table.

As a kid, she didn't mind her body. She'd gobbled Milky Way Stars and popcorn at the Odeon without even thinking. It started at secondary school, got worse through GCSEs – she'd fucked those up royally. For A levels, she made herself eat. She wanted to go to university. People in the university brochures always looked so happy, tucked into one another. Uni turned out not to be that great though, just slides, and reading lists, and a cafeteria with halogen lighting and tuna fish salad. But she'd met Richard there, and he'd put his arm around her and folded her inside. And she'd smiled, and he'd sat in on her lectures just to be there, holding her hand. It had felt so good.

'Joy, stop punishing me, please.' Is it the therapist who teaches him to say such banal things?

'I'm not,' she says. 'Don't be—' The word she wants is ridiculous, but her tongue flops exhausted to the floor of her mouth. She had this really expensive blue silk dress once – chosen because it was the same colour as the sky in her dreams. But oil spotted the sleeve and then she couldn't wear it any more. It didn't matter if she covered the stain with a cardigan; she still knew it was there. This is what Richard looks like to her now. He just isn't special any more. She can finally stop. There is nothing worth eating for.

'I want to go home.'

He drives her home. She sleeps on and off in the car. Joy's waking hours are decreasing. Each day gets shorter as her personal planet tilts into winter.

He carries her to the bed, princess style. She thinks, I don't love you any more. 'Go away.' He pulls the lip of the sheets up to her neck.

'No,' he says, 'I'm going to save you.'

Who does he think he is?

As he stands by the door about to flick off the light, the bulk of him makes her sick. She liked it once. Richard is heavy. Not fat, but heavy. It made her feel small and seagull-boned. But now, it is just a rind around his centre. Even with her eyes shut, she can see it. Stupid creature sewn of fat, sweat and skin. Why had she expected something better? She has stopped believing in magic wardrobes, and wizard schools; so why persist in believing their love is somehow blessed?

He stands in the doorway watching her. He is still wearing his coat. It is a long coat, down to his ankles. She bought it when the old one fell apart. It was the old coat really, that had caught her eye at uni. Back then, most of the boys wore trackie tops or military surplus lumps or, at best, peacoats bought by their mums. But Richard had this overcoat, brown tweed and long. It reminded you that he had broad shoulders. It had an inner pocket, from which he could pull out a packet of cigarettes or whisky in a flask, the whole thing juxtaposing so prettily with the tumble of his innocent blond hair. It was so easy to imagine the coat draped around her shoulders, she knew just how it would tent her in warmth. She knew just how his knuckles would stroke her neck as he did it and how small and charming she would look. How he'd shiver in the cold, and his nose would be pink when he bent down to kiss her. It was that sort of coat.

The new coat. The new coat. The new coat. It was just the same. No different. She wants to cry or thrash. She betrayed herself when she bought it. She knows now that it is replaceable. The new coat hangs on her husband who hangs in the doorway. She glares and glares until the darkness eats him up.

*

One of Richard's clients has died. Richard fires off instructions to a trainee. He makes himself coffee in the French press. From the kitchen window, he can see all the way over to Inverness, a grey ridge near the Firth. He knows that at night, the city lights will streak the sky. He stands by the window looking out at the water. The coffee is good. A small happiness flaps across his vision, and then is gone. There is work to do.

He fires off another email. Business doesn't stop for death. There are always executors to be notified. If Joy dies, he'll have to change his own will. His own parents don't need the money. He and Joy have no children. He gave up on children long before this relapse. His sister married an Indian guy. At the christening, everyone gathered around the kid, desperately pointing out how maybe she had Richard's nose or Aunt Mabel's eyes, like people identifying bodies after a fire. Richard wondered what his and Joy's baby would look like. Where would the Chang genes triumph and where would his push through? That day, Joy had whispered in his ear that she was glad they'd never have kids.

Perhaps he'll leave everything to this niece.

It is late when Richard makes his way upstairs. He touches the brass door handle as tenderly as if it were a lock of Joy's hair, letting his hand rest for a second. Then he eases the door open.

She lies on the plinth of the bed; somehow the blankets have fallen off. She looks like an origami girl, all sharp corners. Is it racist to think of a Chinese girl as origami? Perhaps his sister would say so? But he means really that he is afraid to touch her for fear of crumpling. Earlier she was talking about unicorns. Weren't they attracted to virgins? What would a unicorn think of those surgeries you could get now? He thinks of the bald nub of Joy's pubic bone, featureless as the wrong side of a telephone handset. If it is possible to revirginise, she has. This line of thought is mad. He wonders is it possible to have sympathetic insanity, the way some men have sympathetic pregnancies?

He removes the honey from his bag. He tries to see how far the level has gone down. How much of this golden-vigour has he snuck into her? A millimetre?

When Joy wakes, the moon is icing-sugar white. The problem with sleeping early is that your body begins to ignore the stars. She is always tired and still she cannot sleep. There is something she has forgotten. Recently, her short-term memory has been blipping in and out. She reaches for the thought, but it slips away. There is something about the pale moon that reminds her of it. Carefully, she slides her legs over the edge of the bed. When was the last time she wanted to look at the moon? She can't remember. She remembers her mother used to say a rabbit lives on the moon, but as a girl she could never make it out. No. No rabbit. She does not even have to stand. The room is small and the bed is close. She presses one hand against the glass to support herself.

The unicorn is looking up at her. Somehow she forgot about it – him. But it is a unicorn, a real unicorn. How could she forget? Richard behind her. She can feel the way the mattress tilts to accommodate him. The unicorn's horn points at her like a long finger. She knows it is selecting her, not her husband. She must stand without help. Getting out of bed is difficult, but she manages. The wallpaper accepts her touch. When she reaches the stairs, she slides down on her bottom, the way she did as a girl – indoor tobogganing. It hurts – each stair edge jabs her – but she often hurts.

In the kitchen. Why is she in the kitchen? It has been a long while since she wanted to grasp time. But she knows there is something she wants to remember. Re-member. Member. Richard fucking that woman. His *member* going in and out and in and out. In her mind's ear, she hears the squelch of body on body. It is hard to remember why she is here. Where are they again? Scotland. Didn't Richard fuck her on that table once? On their honeymoon. Her feet wrapped around the bulk of him. Outside, birds chattered – gossiping about them, she'd joked. Outside. Joy remembers there is a unicorn outside.

Richard has left the sugar bowl on the table. In it, the grains are bright. She licks her pinky, and presses into the demerara. When it lifts off, the finger is sugar-studded. Then she sucks. It tastes warm. She only wants enough to make it outside. She will not tell Richard about this. It is not good to show signs of giving in. She does not hate him that much. She will save him from false hope.

She opens the door. The air tastes purple. The unicorn is there. He is not very pretty. Off-white, like the sagging bathroom ceiling; aged plaster coloured by condensation and years of sloughed-off skin. The flanks are slabs.

A unicorn.

No matter how stubby the horn, it is impossible to erase the magic. Pine needles are caught in the mane. Where was the creature when she was in the bath? Did the same breeze blow across them both? The wind is blowing again, and she leans against the doorway. The unicorn's eyes are black. Its lashes are black. But then, so is everything; Joy has to shut her eyes and sit down. This weakness is absurd. Who shuts their eyes looking at a unicorn? She opens them, but the creature has left her. The doormat bristles scratch. For the first time, she registers that she is naked, but she doesn't have the energy to turn back. The gravel gnaws her feet as she lurches forwards.

When he wakes up, Joy isn't in the bed. She hasn't even left a dent. He shivers. Cold has wound around his body. He shakes it off as he stands.

'Joy? Joy!' The door to the room is open. He is not alarmed, not yet. Has she tripped? Overestimated her own strength? The bathroom is innocent, the tub drained of water and bodies. Downstairs, he sees the door is open. He shoves his feet into his shoes. Maybe this is why she is abandoning him – he remembers to put on his shoes. It seems callous. He can't stop doing this, coming up with new reasons.

'Joy? Joy?' There are no street lights here. The moon dusts the empty driveway. Moonlight. Romantic, right? 'Joy, where the fuck are you? This isn't funny.' He sounds like his mum. There is a torch hanging by the doorway and he grabs it. The rubber button gives a businesslike click. Light cuts a circle onto the grass. Bugs move in the beam. He catches grass in the act of pushing up through pebbles. 'Joy?' He is shouting. There are no neighbours to complain; there are also no neighbours to ask, have you seen my wife? Gravel laughs at him. Wind is blowing through trees and he hears the gasping of leaves.

He almost doesn't see her. Her pale body is wrapped against the fence post, at the far end of the drive. Mindlessly, he runs.

'Gone away,' she says.

'I'm right here.'

He has no jacket and nothing to wrap her in. Her bones cut triangular shadows from the torch's light, sharp as sharks' teeth. The hair that grows all over her body glows softly. These fine white hairs grew denser while the hair of her head blew away. They appeared in clumps like mould on bread. She stands, spine sloped, toes splayed to support herself.

'Not you,' she says.

'We're going home.'

Her body is cold against his chest. In the kitchen, he makes tea, with full fat milk and two hillocks of sugar. She drinks it. He has to hold the base of the mug, so that she can lap at it like a cat, but she drinks it. She doesn't complain. Her tongue is grey. Her teeth are grey. He cannot remember an image of her that has made him happier than his wife drinking tea.

'Thank you,' he says. He tries to say it slow and deep, but gentle too. She ignores him, and keeps drinking. He is content with the sight of her, her whole body curved around the goal of filling itself. He doesn't know what happened out in the dark. But she wants to get better. Things are going to get better. He can feel it.

The next day, Joy accepts the spoons of yoghurt, opening her mouth like a baby. He refrains from making the aeroplane noises he has seen his sister use to tempt the niece. Joy smiles at him and yoghurt lines the creases in her too-thin lips. Is it really going to be this easy?

'I thought we could go to the birds of prey show.'

'Mmm.'

She is blanched as the white yoghurt wobbling on the spoon, and yet he hopes. Five years ago, she sat in that chair, she leant across the table and hooked her fingers around his ear, moved them around his neck. Oh. Oh. Oh. His friends thought she was high maintenance, they didn't understand why he put up with it. But the way she'd looked at him.

After she got sick, one or two took him aside and suggested, 'These days, it's until courts do us part, mate.' They weren't the sort of men who said mate, but it was as if they needed a rougher-hewn vocabulary to express this thing. He doesn't do divorces, not for himself and not professionally.

Joy is looking out the window. Her eyes dart from one detail to the next. It has been so long since her eyes wanted to distinguish one thing from the next. He reaches out and puts a hand around hers.

At the Owls, Hawks and Eagles exhibition, the handler brings out a speckled brown bird. It looks a lot like the other brown birds that have come before it, that have ducked and dived for their pleasure.

'This is Harris the Hen Harrier Hawk. He's endangered. Do you know why he's endangered?'

The crowd is small, old people, and two 7-Up-gulping kids near the front who shake their heads.

'The grouse moors are persecuting this guy. He just wants a little bit of dinner. Isn't that right, Harry?'

The hawk soundlessly opens its beak, flexing the black scythe.

'How about we give him some dinner?' The kids clap. The yellow chick arcs upwards from the keeper's leather glove. It is already dead. Can Harris tell? Richard turns to watch Joy watch. It is by her smile that he knows the bird has caught its food.

'Do you think anyone here would notice if it went extinct? Like that guy?' He points to the father of the 7-Up-swallowers. 'Would he call his friends at Proctor & Gamble and weep down the line – did you hear the Harrier Hawks are gone?' Richard asks. This is the sort of comment that used to make her laugh and they would snuggle together in cosy superiority – together against the hypocritical world. Her smile drops.

'Everything is more precious just before it vanishes,' she says. The words come out slowly, and it is hard to tell if this is a rhetorical choice or just physical impairment.

'What do you mean?' he asks. But she's gone back to watching the harrier, so he tries to fill in. 'I guess we'd feel rather different about polar bears if kids were being mauled on Ken High Street.' She doesn't laugh.

After the birds, Joy wants to see the horses. Richard has never liked horses. It is impossible to look them in the eye. The paddock is churned to dirt. It smells of horseshit. She stares for a long time at a white one, whose face reminds Richard of nothing so much as a long skull.

'I want to walk to the car,' she says.

Cold shakes Joy's bones. This is Scotland. Of course it is cold. She is always cold. This is why her husband has to wrap her in two jumpers – an inner and an outer. But this is a deeper cold. Her hands are sweating. They are sticky. She balls her fists. This weakness isn't fair. It isn't. She is eating. She is getting well. Next time, she will be able to follow the unicorn. She will be able to follow this actually special thing. She was wrong to think Richard was anything unique. Men let women down all the time. She's never heard of a unicorn letting anyone down. She wills her spine to be strong. She is good at willpower. Her abstinence was firm – she must be firm in her recovery.

'I want to walk to the car,' she repeats.

'You can't.'

'It's not far.'

She stands and puts her hands in the air, like she's been blessed, like it's a miracle.

'The lame can walk,' she says. But as she laughs, she stumbles and falls back into her seat. She cannot look at him as he pushes the chair to the Kia or as he lifts her and straps her in. She sees only his hairy hands, and hates them. They press her own.

'You're hot.'

'No, I'm not.'

He touches her forehead. 'You have a fever.' His hand feels like a wodge of ice.

'I'm fine.'

'We should get you to a doctor.'

The hospital recited lists of ways in which starvation can damage: bacterial infection, viruses and heart problems, and it never seemed that bad. Only now does she feel the threat of the list. She doesn't have time for the hospital. She doesn't have time for tubes, or concerned nurses, or thermometers, or mandatory weigh-ins. Unicorns do not wait.

'I'm fine.'

'No you're not. I'm taking you to the hospital.'

'No, no, no.' She grips the seat belt like a child. Children make do with the little power they have, she thinks. She was a smart child. She opens her eyes wide. 'You said this was a holiday, just for the two of us. You promised.'

'Fine then. When we get back to London.'

She can't remember when that is. How long have they been here? He is touching her face. She supposes she has been harsh before. As faces go his is as well made as any other. It is just that she feels nothing for it. Not even anger. To feel fury you have to give a damn. She supposes she was angry before. But now she feels nothing. When Harris the Hen Harrier Hawk caught the chick in its mouth, she knew that a small life had been lost. Lungs had been crushed, tiny stomach torn, legs bent and broken. But really, she knew that no one cared about the chick. It was just a chick like any other and Richard was just a man like any other. No, her business now is the Unicorn. And the Unicorn is not in London.

'When?' she says. Richard pulls the car to the side of the road. No, this is not what she meant at all. It was not supposed to be encouragement. He takes out his mobile. He finds the number quickly – the doctor is saved to his contacts. The appointment he makes is for tomorrow afternoon. How can they be leaving tomorrow?

He begins to carry her upstairs to bed. But she doesn't want to sleep.

'Dinner please?'

'Of course.' He pulls her closer to him. She can feel his lungs deflating and inflating, through his shirt. His organs are obscene. Far more than her own. She wonders how she can have wanted this person.

Richard leaves Joy in the cottage, in a big tartan chair from which she has promised not to move. It will not do for her to eat the Pot Noodle he was planning on for his dinner. She has refused the hospital-endorsed weight gain drink. She wants *real food*. He has to cook something gentle, something that won't upset her stomach. Nothing with e-numbers, something that is pure health.

The Tesco is huge. It feels disproportionate for the landscape, rearing up more castle-like than the castle. Standing before row upon row declaring: FEMININE HYGIENE, HOUSEHOLD CLEANING, TEA, COFFEE, CRISPS, DAIRY, MEAT, he realises he has no idea what to make.

In the past, it was Joy who cooked. She used to measure

out oils and sugars in little silver measuring spoons. She was precise. She weighed things on a gleaming kitchen scale. She owned lots of 'Clean Eating' books. Until he met her, Richard wasn't aware that so many foods were dirty. But she was on trend, of the moment. 'You're a good cook for a skinny girl.' Which of his friends had said that?

He looks on his phone for recipes. Can she really digest a salad? An avocado he thinks, avocados are soft. If he were her, he'd want an avocado.

He can do this.

She waits until Richard is out to unclench her hands. Her nails have dented the skin. She is pleased. At least her nails are strong. She thinks she shouldn't have bitten the nurse who shoved the terrible liquid up her nose. She is alive for this. She looks at the wall clock. She wonders how long Richard will be gone. Unicorns are scared of men, she knows that. Unicorns are on to something.

She stands. Now that Richard is not here to distract her, she can do it.

The sitting-room door is close. Five steps away, she thinks. It turns out to be six and she has to hold the frame. The effort buckles her. One, two, three, four, five, six, seven, eight, nine, ten, eleven, twelve steps and she makes it down the insipid hall with its framed prints of deer on blurry moors. She shoves her feet into Richard's leather-lined loafers. Her own are too fiddly and she is afraid that if she lowers herself to them, she will not stand up again. These are designer of some kind, but neither of them brought wellies; they didn't imagine going on hikes.

The road goes towards a wood to her left and a farm to her right. Out in front is a field. The sun snivels weakly behind white cloud. Dirty sheep mooch on the muddy grass. There is nothing here. This is just some shitty countryside, in a country that is just as empty of wonder as the nation to its south. The road sign is dented and tells her only that this is a passing place. Aren't all places passing places? She hopes so. What was she expecting? A sign that said *Unicorn This Way*?

Joy feels fear. It is cold as a forgotten bath. She is sinking deeper and deeper into the enamelled horror. She is crazy. This is why they send you to psychiatrists, because you are crazy. This is why they hold your hand and carefully explain that you cannot go on a hunger strike just because your husband fucks another woman.

She walks towards the wood. She can feel the fever in her knees. It is eating up the back of her spine. The sheep turn their black faces towards her, but who are they to judge? In the distance, spots of cars skid along a highway.

One, two, three, seven, twenty, thirty-one, the wood is further than it looks. On the Moray Firth, oil rigs stick ruddy fingers up from the deep. This is the countryside but it is all new, all modern. Phone masts spindle the fields. Unicorns don't live in places like this. But now, it is how many steps home? She doesn't know. The fever is suffocating her. But she licks her sweaty palm and the sweat is salt-sweet. She keeps going.

The trees are spaced further apart than they looked from the road. These are beech trees, although she thinks she sees pine deeper in. Little yellow mushrooms push up from the ground. She ate those once she thinks, in a restaurant in Soho. Richard took her with his friends. Everything was cooked in butter. Underfoot, the earth mutters. She leans against a tree and sees below her hand a slug, thick as her pinkie. She will never make it home. She doesn't care. Richard will look for her. She, too, was chasing something. What was she looking for? She found something good, but now she can't remember what it is.

The slug's antennae move in and out. She smiles down at it. The slug moves slowly, heaving along the grey-brown bark. It is such a bright thing really. Why call lazy people slugs? It is such an industrious beast. It is so soft, so easily torn or smeared in yellow blood, and yet here it is moving slowly, upwards. Eating and breathing with such a limited frame. She forgets that she is cold. She forgets that she is shaking. The slug moves forward on its silent mouth. She feels good. Her body wants to sleep and the ground is soft. The earth is warm. Even the poking beechnuts feel fond. The smell of moss creeps along the air. The sun fingers the leaves. Time moves on its creaking legs. She lets it step over her.

She doesn't hear the unicorn until it is in front of her. She feels the muzzle press against her cheek. It is warm. Its mouth is grey. Its teeth are long and yellow. The hair is stiff. It has lowered itself on its bony knees. The nose pushes against her stomach. It is here for her. She reaches up and puts her hands on the high cheeks.

She presses her nose to the mane. Mucus clusters around the unicorn's eye. *Unicorn mucus*, even that sounds special. The nostrils are bright with snot. But this too is good. This is no glass horse. This is alive. The slime of life!

The sun is low and gone. The trees wiggle dark fingers. In the distance, the city gilds the Firth's shore. Joy heaves herself up, using the animal as a ladder. It accepts her grip without complaint. Her hips click as she straddles the creature's back. Her face falls against the mane and his hair catches in her nostrils. She holds on tight. His neck is as thick as a man's chest. It smells of woods and heat. It smells also of that feeling that blows across London some August nights when she feels the city and the forest are not separate things but one long sprawl of life. And together they are moving now, faster and faster.

Richard pulls up the driveway. As his eyes meet the golden eyes of the cottage, he pats the groceries at his side. He opens the door. When he calls her name, he feels it humming through him. 'Joy!' he says. 'Joy! I'm home!'

Pragma

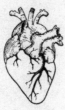

From Ancient Greek

prag- do or practise; ma-, Greek noun; also Hellenistic Greek adjective 'relating to fact'

A longstanding love; a deeper, mature under-standing; love that endures and is logical. Literal translation also means what is done: a deed, or a fact.

Pragma is love that is linked to time, that stands still and endures. There's no falling in love here; rather, it is about a lack of movement. Though it can refer to a practical, rational love, it is also tied up in a love that is simply constant.

One More Thing Coming Undone

D.W. Wilson

One night not too long ago I came home from a bad highway crash muddied by swampwater and found that an ancient Camaro had fishtailed onto my front lawn. Sharkskin blue, half a century young, all angles and testosterone and elbows draped out the window – a real hellbender's ride. I parked my half-ton beside it. Raindrops big as lug nuts pelted my windshield and hood in equal measure, and down the street the water pooled like floodplain at the sewers. A vintage car shouldn't have survived in that weather, but the Camaro had no rust in her wheel wells and her paint job shone. The inside was upholstered in Naugahyde – a vinyl straight from the Age of Aquarius – and a pine air-freshener swayed from the rear-view alongside a loop of prayer beads and some dog tags whose origins I did not know.

In my half-ton I wiped mud and fatigue from my eyes and I imagined all the places that Camaro might take me, and all the places it already had: some deserted theme park in northern Alberta where, for a moment in my twenties, I felt older than I do now; Cawker City's legendary ball of twine, largest in the world; my dad's funeral. The bones in my hand ached – old injury, a divining rod for trouble. See, I knew who that car belonged to, and I knew the ruin that followed in his wake. Some people damage whatever they touch, but others save the worst for their friends.

At the house's rear door I unlaced my steeltoes and left them for the elements, then I went inside and followed the hallway to the kitchen where I found him at the table with a beer in one hand and a banana in the other. Face like a pug and poodle cross, Red Army beret slanted to the right: Animal Brooks, my once best friend, back in my life after two decades gone.

With his toe, he nudged a six pack at the base of his chair. Mud oozed off me whenever I shifted. It gummed my hair and stuck like grit to my teeth, a taste more sulphur than dirt, like a peatbog with hints of its long-entombed dead. Animal scanned me head to toe, but didn't react. As far as I knew, nothing had ever fazed him.

It's good to see you, Duncan.

Fuck me, I said.

He wore maroon Carhartt overalls and combat boots rubbed through the arches – exactly as I remembered him, exactly as I'd last seen him. His hands picked at the kitchen table, the tab of his beer, the frayed hem of his off-white shirt. Antsy, a fidgeter: he used to say that nobody'd catch him sitting still unless he died. When he vanished, not long after I graduated high school, the whole town felt his absence, like when somebody cuts the music at a party. On and off, you'd hear a rumour about a drag racer in a vintage Camaro who shook the police in Hamilton, or some maniac communist on an oil rig who shanked a man with his own broken rib. *Animal*, the rumour-whisperer always added, under his breath. *Animal*.

At my table, he made a wet, croaking sound – half cough, half gag, like somebody who'd whiffed rotten eggs.

You okay? I said.

Just peachy, he said, almost voiceless. With the banana peel, he dabbed phlegm from the squint of his mouth. Twenty-two years earlier he stowed away on the belly of a coal train and gunned east for the Promised Land. *Come with me*, he'd said, and traced this dent in his forehead most people blamed on a cow's hoof. *Come with me, D-Man*. No notice: just rolled up at the welding yard, commie hat askew, a hiker's pack one-shouldered. *I'm getting out. We're getting out*.

Now, dark moons hollowed his cheeks and wrinkles edged his lips to a frown. His face looked as though it had chinned a lot of cold air. Life of drugs and drink, maybe, life of sleeping rough. I knew what to look for. Travel back in time not ten years, before I met my wife, Audrey, and you'd find me in Animal's camp.

I leaned on the fridge, left a muddy silhouette. Still got your Camaro.

He flexed one cheek, windmilled his tongue as if to spit. You can have her, if you want her.

I don't.

Look at you, he said. Mister high and fucking mighty.

Who told you where I live? I said. Who let you in?

He reached between his knees for a beer and hooked his thumb in one of those plastic hoops known to strangle gulls. Dark water pearled off me like a coffee drip, so while Animal plucked at the beer's tab, I went to the laundry room. There, I trashed my T-shirt and bent over the plastic basin to scour dirt from my arms. Parcels of muck and cattail swirled down the drain and I smelled the eggy stink of phosphorus. Earlier, on the rain-blind highway, this horse trailer in front of me had lurched over the meridian and down an embankment, and I stopped to save the driver. He'd broadsided the marsh, and in the middle of all that fuel and metal I discovered one of the beasts strung up in the branches of an evergreen, splay-limbed like some kind of horse Jesus.

Animal appeared next to me. With his beer can, he gestured at the scar across my ribs – a dozen weals of pink tissue, haphazard like thrown bones. What're those? he said.

I rolled my shoulders in their sockets and maybe the knots loosened. Without meaning to, my fingers grazed my chest. Animal's eyes followed them, seemed to size me up in the process. He'd gone east and lived a life of never-look-twice adventures everybody else just dreamed about. Twenty-two years and no attempt at contact, not with anyone – or, at least, not with me. Under the low amber light he looked incorporeal, more memory than man.

Can I grab ya a brewski? he said.

Why are you here? I wanted to say. Instead, I told him to get me a Coke and a Robax from the kitchen. In his absence I cranked the hot tap and gulped clouds of vapour and coughed whoops of muddy water. In my mind I saw the truck and trailer at the instant of its descent, jackknifed mid-air with its loading door flung wide and the horse eyes big and marbled as a bruised knuckle. It took all my resolve not to drive by that wreck and those animals shitting through their death rattles. But I couldn't do it. The driver might've been a foot-ball coach, or a dad. He was unconscious and drowning in the cab. Rain so heavy it weighed my arms down. Thunder like the great warping of sheet metal. I put an elbow through the window.

My watch said two-twenty in the morning and the ther-mometer said thirty-six. The downpour on my yard splashed chutes in the air – groundwater at saturation – and the wind eddied across it. Most of us had abandoned our basements and sandbagged our front doors. Electrical storms wailed nonstop on BC's interior and hailstones like spruce bugs pummelled the West Coast. A thousand fish had washed ashore at Kitamaat, driftwood-rigid, and people whispered about glacial thaw and that a huge wave would sweep Vancouver into the sea.

Animal returned without a Coke. In his hands: an opened can of nondescript lager, a tiny pill. I placed the muscle relaxant in my mouth and washed it down. He watched me do it, this look on his face as if I'd failed a test, but I'd given up living with pain. My spine had never recovered from a disc I slipped widebacking a floor joist, years before. Getting older is getting achier. Yeah, my doctor told me, when I went in to see him, not too long ago. You're forty-one. You ache now.

I gotta ask something, Animal said, and tried to lay his palm on my shoulder, but I swatted him away. Did you love Vic Crane?

I felt every inch of my skin. I felt the weight of my own tongue.

Why'd you leave? he said. You were everything to her.

Steam rose from the basin and I scrubbed water over my arms until the sediment had sloughed off them. Animal's beer tasted like sod so I emptied it down the drain. Across the street, a neighbour's security lamp yellowed my lawn like an old photo. A bicycle had been kicked over by the wind, along with a bunch of stupid toys we should've hauled indoors – inflatable dog, two neoprene Slip 'n' Slides, technicoloured water guns. The laundry room smelled of damp cotton and beer and sweat and the oniony, claustrophobic scent of men.

I let myself think about Vic Crane, then, which I'd spent a decade training myself not to do. I remembered her arms strong as lasso and her neon hair and freckles and a lazy eye and a filthy laugh that made me so crazy in love with her, and for a moment I went someplace else: Invermere BC at the start of the new millennium – high school behind us and the whole world wide open, our endless drinking and heartache.

Fuck you, Animal, I managed, but he'd slumped unconscious against the wall, knees at his ears and hands on the floor. His spilled beer stained the carpet straw.

I walked outside in my socks and lifted my arms to let the weather have its way with me, and when lightning flashed it etched Vic's face on the clouds. The rain tasted of dirt and smoke but more flavours, too, which couldn't have been there: cinnamon, and sandalwood, and thyme – shades of a girl's perfume. Far off, the Rocky Mountains sawtoothed the western horizon. You don't realise it, but the past is right behind you, all the time.

Later, after I'd stripped down and dried off, I dragged a blanket from the closet and flung it over Animal, and I went to the bedroom and listened to Audrey dream and I thought about our past and the pasts we had before we had each other. Audrey slept with a wet cloth around her ankles, and these had gone lukewarm and inked two circles on the bed, so I tugged them loose and took them to the bathroom to make them once more cold. These gestures are important, even when they go unnoticed. I laid the cloths on her ankles, touched her cheek, a divot near her ear from a stray welding spark. She smelled like ginger and Imperial Leather and she was hot as a bath – a defence mechanism, we joked – but I didn't join her. Instead, I stooped by the window while rain bent our trees like car antennas. I checked on our daughter. We wouldn't have regrets if we didn't have memories, but then, I guess, we wouldn't have memories.

In the bleeding hours of the morning, sleepless, I shoved two cups of coffee down my gullet and stared for a long time at the keys in my palm. To stall her, I switched off the alarm clock and wound Audrey's watch back an hour, and without waking her or Animal Brooks or leaving a note, I went out the door and rolled down the driveway in neutral and began the five-hour drive from Kirkwall to Invermere, and to Vic.

Emergency crews had erected a big sign that flashed cautions about washouts and mudslides and that they couldn't guarantee rescue. Infrequent cell reception, unstable roads. In fluorescent yellow: *be prepared*. I drove over the rumblestrip to the shoulder and killed the ignition but left the radio on, and with nineties power ballads angsting from the speakers I let myself stew in the shadow of the Rockies.

Twelve years building a life without her. I got out and sat on the tailgate. The storm had eased and the scent of wet pine rose around me. It smacked of open fires in my dad's yard, or summers at a cabin on Lethe Lake, me and Vic and her dad and her dad's dog – a two-legged pug named Bipug. I grew up like that, dirty-jeaned and covered in the Stuff of Nature. We met because Vic got stuck in a tree, and my dad owned a ladder. I can still see her skinny legs all nicked and scraped from where she'd shimmied along the trunk, a ballcap with her ponytail through the clasp, nine years old. My dad invited them over. We drank Minute Maid.

Headlights crested a hill on the highway home. A car, clipping my way. I reached through the rear window and flicked my hazards. On roadtrips, in the evening, me and Vic used to haul over to the gravel and sit shoulder to shoulder and share JD and belt one another in the charlie horse. Afterwards, thighs blueing like eggplants, we'd roll out a couple of foamies and lay down and watch stars wheel above us. Me and Audrey don't do that. She prefers a tent's canvas, the insulated walls of our home. I got her pregnant a month after the wedding.

The car signalled, chewed to the shoulder, turned down. Animal in that fucking Camaro.

Left without me, he hollered.

Christ, I said.

He stepped out and knocked his boots together. A fresh yoke of beer hung from his fist and he swung it in a deliberate arc. Behind him, the horizon boiled with clouds the colour of rusted tin. Red sky in the morning, and all that jazz. That thing burns too much gas, he said, and jerked his thumb at the Camaro. Can't afford to follow you.

Can't afford much? I said.

Live as though it's better days.

He leaned on the sky-coloured hood, crossed his arms. If I'm honest, he didn't look great. Under the pale light of morning, his skin had no lustre to speak of, and I could see the salmony underside of his eyelids. Soft, shrunken, a ghost of the man I once knew. It'd been twenty some years, sure, but how long is that?

What's this about, Animal?

Same thing it's always been about, D-Man.

Me and Vic?

Saying her name made me shiver, like when you know someone's about to touch you. My thoughts of her were in

33

full swing – fist-sized breasts and stonewashed jeans and a body of pure rope, her no-bullshit-or-else way of things. You could count on one hand our days apart through high school. She saved me from drowning, in grade ten – dove into the Sevenhead against all orders and trawled me from the rapids and breathed the air back in, so I woke tasting her lips like life. Talking about her, thinking about her – I'd forgotten the experience.

Animal dragged himself onto the tailgate. We squinted at the sun.

Is she sick?

No, Animal said. Then: I don't know.

A breeze shucked along the highway, moist with the scent of soil. Animal pressed his tongue to a canine, polished and polished the enamel. I checked the time: five-twenty-four in the morning. In a few hours Audrey would wake and find me gone and she'd make the assumption she had every reason to make. *He went to work early*, she might tell our daughter, twist a grey hair behind her ear, stare at the plain yard and our plain house and wonder how and why she ever ended up right there, right then. *He'll be home soon.*

You pretty much owe it to her, D-man.

Don't you think I know that?

He tore a beer free of the pack, cracked it and took an overlong slurp, offered a go-to shrug. To the east – homeward – the sun nudged over the horizon, a rare shellac of colour. Clouds were sweeping in from the south and, on the radio, the weatherman crooned soothsayings about glutted rivers and breached dykes and that a three-hundred-foot tidal wave had creamed the western seaboard.

I folded into the driver's seat and Animal was already riding shotgun. My hand went to the ignition, my foot cycled the clutch. The truck quaked beneath me and I traced each judder as it cambered up my shins and hips and spine and out to my arms and hands and through my palms slick on the wheel and down the steering column to the undercarriage, the brake pads, tyre treads, only to rise and start all over again. And through it all this vision of a girl with purple hair and her shirt bunched at her chin, half-naked on a beach, or under a duvet, or in a sleeping bag on a bed of cattail, or at high noon on a floating living room on a floodplain, the heat of her in my hands, sweat – hers, mine – like ethanol. They say your first love is the most intense and the most lasting, but maybe it just takes the most from you, leaves the biggest hole.

The truck jerked to first gear and the highway unfurled, and when I pressed the throttle and the gasp of acceleration clinched the seat belt taut, it was as if I was cheating on Audrey – a total physical awareness that dimmed moment by moment, like when you submerge in a lake and the cold plucks your skin, but after a while you don't feel the water any more, only the unnatural – but not *wrong*, not *bad* – weightlessness, and exhilaration.

The air in Invermere hung with that gummy taste of asphalt – a pressure more than a flavour, like catarrh. Animal had spoken maybe a dozen words the whole drive but he'd polished off half as many beers. The empties piled at his feet until one by one he deposited them into the truck bed. A few spittoons fell from the sky, enough for me to set my wipers low.

We passed the bakery with its pretzel sign big as a stallion. We passed the arena where I once took part in a no-holds-barred battle royal and shattered all the bones in my hand. Animal patted the dashboard, the still mud-damp seat, flicked the pine freshener with the gnawed-on nail of his middle finger. This is a nice truck, he said. What'd it damage you? Fifty grand? A hundred?

I rebuilt it, I said. From a wreck.

Anyone die?

Yeah, I said. My mom.

Shit, Animal said. Dying sucks.

As I drove, muscle memory took the wheel. My arms tugged left and right around curves and potholes I'd long forgotten and not seen. Ten years away, but I swear. I clocked a few of me and Vic's hangouts: a playground's giant octopus – now sunk a metre in the ground – that we used to cuddle in and smoke dope; the copper roof of an old guy's house, rusted dark as moss, where we sat and drank while the sun rose like an hour hand over the Rockies.

The rain came harder. Animal directed me to a timber-frame bungalow with a roof the colour of lodestone. It was the house he'd always owned – passed down from his grandmother – and the first place I lived away from home, for one hundred and fifty bucks a month. A long time ago its backyard opened onto floodplain from the Sevenhead, but now the wetland had receded, and fifty feet from the porch you arrived at a gully of cracked ground and chaff. Vic warned us all about that. In high school, she used words like *desertification* and *arid lands,* and she talked about bigger things and better places, about how small the valley was and how you had to get out or else it'd keep you, forever. I'm scared of getting stuck, Duncan, Vic once said to me, and clamped her small, strong hand on my bicep. I'm sick of looking *up*.

I parked in the bungalow's gravel driveway and clocked movement through the front window, a flash of plaid. My mouth went dry. Animal shouldered open his door and dropped to the moist earth. He tossed a wave in my direction and cut across the tailgate and out of sight behind a mobile home. I waited for him to reappear until it became clear he wouldn't: gone as suddenly, and as wholly, as he'd arrived. Not his fight, I guess, and not his area of expertise, relationships. In the house, a light flicked on and a light flicked off. Near the front door, a Coke-bottle wind chime clanged – school art project, or something salvaged.

She opened the door before I mounted the steps. Logging coat worn unbuttoned, no neon hair, a white tank top and jeans scuffed in half-moons at the thighs, dimples that raised her mouth to a smile. Her hair hung longer than I'd ever seen it – below the shoulders, slashed here and there with a grey that looked silver among the blond. The years had been kinder to her than they had to me: she'd acquired hips, a delicate raking of wrinkles. I didn't know what I felt or what I should feel. Of course I loved Vic Crane, Animal, you stupid fuck.

She crossed her arms and leaned on the doorframe, teen-ager-style, and I saw the pinch where bicep met chest and I saw her abbreviated ring-finger, knob-ended at the first joint. Snipped it off herself, the year I left, while doped out of her mind on PCP. Her dad told me about it. Bolt cutters. *How much you fucking dare me?*

Vic nodded at my truck. Bio-diesel, she said, stressing every *b*, every *d*. Hybrid. Reduced emission combustion. Duncan Jones. Look at you.

You know me, Vic.

But do I? You've turned Green.

I even vote for them. Maybe you got through to me.

Two decades in hiding. How little it takes to change a man.

Her front yard wasn't seeded and the topsoil, even under a brief downpour, thickened like stew. I didn't know what to do with my hands so I shoved them in my pockets. Overhead, storm clouds darkened the sky. Soon there'd be thunder, maybe lightning. No matter how you spun it, I'd be a fool to risk the highway home.

Vic smacked her palm on the timber. You here alone? she said.

Well, Animal's gone.

Her shoulders fell an inch. I know, she whispered. It's sad.

She came down the stairs and stopped at arm's length. That close, I could see all the details my mind had let slip: her half-grin that showed both rows of teeth, the discolouration in one iris, skin that shone as though she'd biked a hill to get to me and only had time to towel dry. She gave me a head-to-toe, made a noise, a *hmph*. When Vic looked at you she had this way of making you feel like you believed in something.

You've been drinking, she said.

No.

You reek of it.

It's in the truck.

She gave me this look, as if to say, *Really, Duncan?* All eyebrows and crossed arms.

With a nod, she retread the steps. I didn't climb after her, not immediately. At home Audrey would be fixing Saturday brunch for our daughter, doing her damnedest not to let resentment eke into the eggs and the toast and the juice. I swear to God, it was like having two hearts.

Eastward, the skies churned in a wind cauldron, dark as fresh cement, and tendrils of rain columned like smoke to the earth. The last time I saw Vic was on a sailing trip around the Gulf Islands, when she and Animal and I bore witness to an arcus cloud – this huge cylinder that cut the sky in two, like a horizon before the horizon. We limped to port at some tiny island as the seas went white, and we spent three days in a room above a pub, the lot of us, drunk on the absurdity of it all.

Vic tapped her fingers on the wood of her door. Come on, then, she said, and I – obediently – followed.

Inside, Vic put me on the couch and plugged in a fan and fished two tumblers and a bottle of bourbon from her liquor cabinet. Around me: evidence of a life lived that I knew nothing about. She had a Scottish flag hung on one wall and a shelf full of objects that looked to me like chunks of shale. I used to live in that house, but she'd knocked down walls and raised others, torn out the shag-carpet we'd all puked on and replaced it with a hemp overlay, and I wondered why she was holed up there, in Animal's house, of all places. Vic lowered herself to a loveseat kiddy corner to me, filled our glasses, and we *tink*ed them together, careful, I suspect, that our fingers did not make contact. I wanted to touch her. I never wanted to touch her. I wanted to remember what it was like to touch her.

The bourbon tasted like flintlock. The fan kicked around an air that smelled like horse blankets. Vic asked me about what I'd been doing in the last two decades and I told her how I'd blown a gasket after we both left the valley, how I drove for days and days from bar to bar and town to town, picking fights. It was all I could think to do – fight – because I could handle a split lip or a fractured wrist. Once, I said, I hit a man so hard with a bar stool his eye came out. I showed her where I'd been shanked with a broken bottle, on the ribs, and how I can't lift my arm above my chest after I dislocated the shoulder going teeth-first over a bandsaw. We drank more bourbon. She said very little. I told her about the pipeline in Northern Alberta, at the tar sands, where I tried to carve myself a niche. Where I tried to die, maybe. I told her about Audrey and how I met her because she'd chained herself to a tree in the pipeline's path. Ten years, I told Vic, since I last made a fist.

She didn't speak for a while. Rain drummed on the roof of her bungalow, loud as a fridge, and the ice cubes in my tumbler jingled on the glass. She pulled the sleeves of her baggy plaid over her hands and bunched the excess fabric in each fist, crossed one leg over the other. Classic pensive pose – we all know it, the one she gives you when you say what you shouldn't say.

Do you miss it? Vic said.

Every day.

Why?

Lightning touched down, not far, its impact tangible in the static lifting of our arm hairs. Vic reached under the coffee table for a glass pipe and a ziplock of weed. It came open with a *vup*, and I smelled the drug's earthy musk, so rich you could almost mistake it for coffee. When she sparked a flame her eyes crossed inward to the cherry and I stared at her and let myself be mesmerised by her until, with a *pop*, the lights went out.

You mind the dark? she said, long exhale.

Not with you, I wanted to say. Instead: Probably won't be out long.

She lit a candle. From the fringe of its glow she told me about her life, about her PhD in environmental biology and the palatial apartment she owned in Edinburgh – or, as she called it, the *Athens of the North* – where she'd studied, and how she almost married an Englishman named Toby Normanton who knew more about fishing than anyone on the living Earth. She'd travelled all over: a stint in Africa to study meerkats and a couple years in Paris, three fateful months down under where, for the first time in her life, her birth control failed. I never told anyone that, she said, and blew smoke out the side of her mouth. I sipped my drink and felt more than tasted the liquid, the subconscious timing of hand to glass to lips and swallow. We were on a kind of cycle, me and Vic, going through the motions. She told me about our high school *mates*, who'd died or had kids or got married – Ash Cooper, Will Crease, the Starman. Names like foreign words on my tongue.

The storm thrashed the roof with a sound like tyres churning gravel. I tasted the cabbage-like funk of marijuana smoke, my own sweat. Vic set her pipe down, took the bourbon by the throat. Let me show you something, she said, and rose. In the darkness I sensed the movement of her body and grabbed for her hand but fanned it. She led me through lightless corridors to her bedroom, where she'd installed a mezzanine with its own little balcony, three-quarters of the way to the ceiling, that overlooked the lifeless marsh. It's covered, she said. Come on, Duncan.

We climbed out and sat side by each with our legs extended. She'd crafted herself a nice nook, girded by the walls of her house. It was the closest we'd been in years. She smelled like better days, like this one time when we walked for hours across a wooden causeway in the middle of that now-dried floodplain, blind in the darkness and the reeds. We got so lost we had to bunk down there on the planks. I gave Vic my coat and she curled onto my chest and we counted the stars and the fireflies and the bioluminescence – a word she taught me that night. In the morning the planks had pressed horizontal imprints into me. With her sleeve, Vic wiped drool off her chin.

On her balcony, Vic broke the silence. That marsh won't ever come back, she said. I'm glad we had it, when we were kids. It was a nice thing to have.

There's a chance it isn't dead, I said.

Duncan, she said. It's science.

Raindrops sputtered off shingles and moistened the hems of our jeans. Vic drank straight from the bottle and I listened to the liquid slosh. It's what we used to do – waste whole days, me and her and no reason to involve anyone else. Maybe hours passed, there on her balcony. Maybe days or aeons or the even longer, ponderous lifetimes of geology. Far away, lightning drew a white line to the mountains.

Why'd you come to see me? she said.

Animal showed up at my house and told me to.

Vic turned the bourbon like an auger. She made a sound, half-*tsk* half-whistle, and gave me a look across her shoulder. The truth was that I hadn't seen Animal in twenty-two years for the same reason I hadn't seen her. Ample opportunity, no follow through. Call it self-preservation. Call it cowardice. That horse, as they say, is out of the barn.

How did Animal die? I said.

Face full of H_2S.

Nobody told me. I saw an obituary. Did you write it?

It would've been like choking on rotten eggs, she said. They make the gas smell that way, on purpose. Fuck, I loved him.

I feel so old, Vic. I feel like my whole life is yesterday.

She shuffled over a few inches. Our thighs brushed. For a second, I'm not sure either she or I knew what would happen. It's possible that in years to come we will both question why that night turned out how it did; like so many moments, it can be added to the column of *might have beens*. Vic rested her head on my shoulder and we dared to let our pinkies touch. A reunion, maybe. Or the start of another goodbye. We are sixteen years old. We are forty-one years old.

Think we get a second chance? Vic said. She offered her palms to the rain.

I hope so, I told her. But I doubt it.

She cleared her throat, coughed a small ribbit into the bourbon. Then she wiped her eye. Liquid down the wrong pipe, I guess.

By accident, I stroked her missing finger, that envelope of skin, and I wondered what it would be like to see a part of you lying there, no longer you, just meat. It must be like wondering what would've happened if you hadn't become a father, or if you'd told a girl how much you loved her, or if you'd packed your bags and ditched your life on a whim and skipped town with your best friend – a strange detachment, as if the past is a thing you can keep in one piece. But who knows. Not me. And not Victoria Crane.

I have a spare room, she said.

Thank you, I wanted to say. Instead: I love you.

Her hand leaves mine. She claps me on the thigh and struggles to her feet. For a second she lingers there half-stooped under the cover of her little balcony, and I like to think she runs through the possibilities: kiss him on the forehead, ruffle his once-thick hair, ask him to leave his wife. But she sets the bourbon down next to me and goes in, and I listen to her footfalls on the ladder and the *caw* of a closing door and the falsetto *shush*ing of the rain. I refill my glass. The storm dumps barrels of water on the marsh but for some reason the marsh stays dry.

*

Later, I woke in the dark on the couch in Vic's living room and blinked through the onset of hangover and I asked myself, really, what I wanted. But in truth I had no idea.

The drive home took me through Biblical downpour and highways so washed out I had to navigate by the grip of my tyres on the asphalt. A Camaro – even Animal's Camaro – could never have done it. I don't know what time I got home or what time I left: in the dressing-down hours of morning, a full day chasing fantasy.

I parked across the street so the engine wouldn't wake my family. Morning shimmered through the bedroom blinds and Audrey lay uncovered to the waist, asleep with a damp cloth on her breasts. I took this from her and she did not stir, and I eased in beside her with my knees in the culvert of her knees. Her naked skin was warm as bread. She smelled like suntan lotion, and I roped an arm around her stomach and my fingers grazed the crescent scar that looped her belly and I tried to figure out how much I loved her. Vic and me used to sleep the same way, and she'd cinch her strong fingers around mine and haul me close, but I couldn't remember what she smelled like or the way she breathed or if I would lie awake next to her and wonder how we'd ever last.

I kissed Audrey between the shoulders and she made a noise, a pleasant grunt. You end up loving people for their habits, for the things they do without knowing. My thumb touched a notch on her spine – a mole she scratched off as a child – and I stroked the tight skin near her ear and the grey hairs that streaked it silver. You end up loving all the things that are not perfect about people. Audrey shifted, her joints circulating blood. I felt the press of her ass and her sander's shoulder curved and tough as a bannister knob. Her hair tickled my nose and I fought not to sneeze and wake her, because she would give me the licking that could wait for day. Maybe you end up loving people for their attitude, for the very way they exist in the world. That's what Vic had that no one else does

– a real way of *doing* things, a real way of *being*. Sometimes, I don't know if our memories live in us or if we live in them.

Audrey's hand cupped my cheek. Her palm roughed over all the bristles.

Duncan? she said, but I didn't answer her. *I'm sorry*, I wanted to say, but couldn't bear to let her hear me. Beads of moisture collected in my eye, probably from the cloth, and I blinked them away. Right then, I'd have given anything to stop wanting Vic Crane so much, but wanting not to want someone is not enough, not on its own. You don't forget the things you wanted, and as you get older their echoes just get louder – lives you nearly led, people you came so close to having, words you rehearsed over and over and over. I can't even be sure Vic would've said, Y*es, Duncan. Yes.*

Audrey put her cheek on my chest and I stroked her hair, scratched my fingernails down her spine. I breathed the smell of her hair, her neck. *I can't love you like I loved Vic*, I wanted to say, but I didn't know how. Outside, the sun hoisted itself above the mountains. Raindrops smacked the window with splashes big as plums. The sky flared orange, a lick of flame to the east.

The unremarkable truth about me and Vic is we petered out – that classic tale about going separate ways, moving on. It's like when you wake from a wicked dream but nobody's out of bed yet, so you sit around and grin at the cat because your dream was so damn fun, and you watch the clock turn-over and you surf TV channels desperate for anyone to stumble from their bedroom. But before anyone gets up and long before the day gets going – Christ, you don't even notice it happen – your dream goes blurry and you forget the best bits, and all you have to show is this vague memory that, a long time ago, you were part of something really, really good.

Philautia

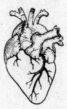

From Hellenistic Greek

phil- love; aut- directed from within, or self

Self-love; a certain regard for oneself; loving yourself; self-obsession

The Greeks divided Philautia into two subsections: narcissism, and an enhancing love for oneself which increased your capacity to love others. This second attitude was favoured most by Aristotle and indicates a self-love that is an achievement; a noble understanding of the self that allows us to form more meaningful friendships with others.

White Wine

Nikesh Shukla

When my sister tells me that her boss referred to her team as his favourite terror cell and her as Bin Laden in an email he had accidentally forwarded to her, we're standing in a supermarket, scanning the shelves for a particular cheap bottle of white wine she has read about on a sommelier blog.

Apparently, it's this season's best supermarket wine.

I keep picking up bottles either I am familiar with (because they're under £6) or ones with an interesting design aesthetic on the label. Rupa shakes her head at each one, fixing her tuts with a reminder that, while sitcoms and the street foods of the world are my domain, we are in her corner of the supermarket.

Eventually, she finds the particular Sauvignon Blanc she is after and picks up three bottles.

We buy them and stand in the doorway of the shop, watching the sky bleed rain, cursing each other for forgetting an umbrella, for timing the booze run so badly.

The security guard makes us take two steps back into the shop so that the automatic doors close. I take the Zadie Smith-branded tote bag from my sister and look at her.

I find it hard to forget I'm her older brother. It defines every atom of our relationship. I can't view her from anywhere other than the paternalistic pedestal I'm on. She looks like she was 19, still. She's wearing a hoodie and tracksuit bottoms we found in boxes we'd unpacked that afternoon, her comfort clothes from university, and she immediately changed. Within seconds, she had gone from Rupa Bhatia, the head of key accounts at a marketing firm to my baby sister, the one whose vomit I had cleaned her first week at university, having picked her up from the union in the middle of the night, and brought her back to Mum and Dad's house because neither of us knew her dorm number. Back then, it was Mum and Dad's house. Home.

Now it's just Dad's bungalow.

'Do you think people can be racist?' she asks me.

I turn to her. The bottles clink in the bag and I automatically readjust the strap on my shoulder.

'How do you mean?' I ask.

She tells me about her boss, a man called Martin, and how he moved her team to near the toilets from their desks by the windows overlooking the river. The desks they'd left were still unoccupied, but he had told Rupa in a meeting, that there had been complaints about the food smells that accompanied their joint packed lunches.

'That sort of smell, well, it's appropriate on a Friday night, after the pub's kicked out and you're in a curry house, but it's not appropriate in a communal office,' he told her.

My sister was confused.

Her team tended to share hummus and crudities, maybe steamed turkey. They were training as a team to do a 10k run for cancer, raising money for the hospice that had looked after Mum, and so were all on training diets.

Later he referred to the team as a terror cell in his email.

Once he sent the email, Rupa tells me, instead of apologising for it, or trying to explain it, he started calling them it to their faces.

'How's my favourite terror cell doing this morning?' he asked, jauntily as he passed their cubicle.

Rupa looked up, unsure she had heard him correctly.

'And their fearless leader, Bin Laden,' he added, before moving on to the next pod over in an adjacent cubicle.

'Rupa,' I told her. 'That's horrendous.'

'I just never really ever believed you,' she told me. 'You and that chip on your shoulder.'

'What do you mean?'

'I know that people used to be racist,' she tells me. 'I just didn't think they still were. It feels so old-fashioned.'

I stare at myself in the mirror.

I'm lying on my side in bed. Dad has kitted this spare room out in flatpack furniture. It feels like rented accommodation. The spotted sheets cover everything but my hot feet. The mirror is part of an empty wardrobe. I think Dad assumes I'll fill it with my things but I intend to only visit for the occasional night every month or so.

Rupa's words haunt me.

She once told me that I carried race too close to my chest, like it was my diary. I replied that she was a self-hating Asian. She refused to see the institutional power structures that keep us in place. She told me I was a self-hating Asian because I refused to engage in my culture. Back then, you were either a freshie or a coconut. There was nothing in-between.

I note the day – it's Saturday, it's June, it's the year my sister has discovered racism. I can hear the television on in the next room so force myself out of bed.

Standing up, my head throbs. White wine headache. Watered down with soda water, much to my sister's annoyance. She winced every time I spritzed up my wine. I took each first sip with a raised eyebrow, looking at her the whole time.

We avoided all conversation about her boss. She asked me not to tell dad. Dad would only make it seem like it was her fault. He's a curious immigrant.

On the one hand, he gave us both the twice-as-good speech, ensuring we knew that anything we turned our hands to, anything we chose to pursue in life, we had to be twice as good as the average white man to have half the opportunities. The country is run by them, he told us both, separately. You have to be better than the average white man. Years later, I realised, most children of immigrants had a version of this

49

speech. This was our burden – to pass on the truth to the next generation until it was no longer needed.

On the other hand, he told me when I relayed an incident where someone called me curry-breath at school, that racism can be quelled through knowledge.

'Son,' he told me. 'Knowledge is power. You can defeat anyone with knowledge. If you have knowledge, you have power. When I worked for Hoover, I knew where all their money was, I knew how to manage their finances, you think anyone said anything racist to me?'

'Dad,' I said. 'That doesn't make any sense. That doesn't mean they're not thinking those things.'

'Why do you care about what is in their head? We think stupid things all of the time. We keep them inside our heads. I do not think this is something to worry about. Knowledge is power.'

'Dad, this is a simplistic way to look at things,' I told him.

'Son, you have a chip on your shoulder. That is what I tell your sister. That you have a chip on your shoulder. And that she must not be like you. Angry. She needs knowledge. She needs to be happy.'

I walk out of the room Dad keeps referring to as mine. I tell him it's his spare room. This makes him upset.

Dad and I eat breakfast with the news on in the background (my request, Dad was watching a cartoon channel when I got up). Rupa is still asleep. I sip painfully at my mug of instant coffee, longing for something that doesn't taste like mud. I watch him pick at his Weetabix, occasionally taking a chilli from the glass bowl next to it, and twirling it around by its tail, watching it dangle.

'You okay, Dad?' I ask.

'I am worried about your sister,' he says.

Dad talks in big declarations. He tends to sound like he is

the first one to have ever had such visceral thoughts as the ones he has.

'She is your sister,' he says, firmly.

I look at him and smile.

'Yes, Dad,' I say. 'You are right. She is.'

I get up from the breakfast counter and walk towards the door of the room she's temporarily living in, while a new kitchen is installed at her house. And a new bathroom. And a new entertainment system. She's fancy, my sister. I went to private school and ended up – with all the access to opportunity – wanting to be an artist. She went to a comprehensive school and, seeing me be given all the opportunity in the world and squander it for the love of words, became a successful award-winning marketing professional.

I knock on the door.

'What?' I hear her call out, groggily.

I ask if she wants a cuppa.

'What?' she calls out again. 'Just open the door.'

I open the door and repeat my question. She turns over in the bed and faces the door. Her hands are over her face. I can't remember who said this, but an old friend told me that all the therapy and well adjustedness in the world is undone the moment you walk back into your teenage home. We're living in the fading glimmer of the existence of ours, and in that moment, seeing a familiar sight – my oversleeping sister groggily refuse to get up until a cup of tea, with two sugars, ends up on her bedside table, I feel overcome with nostalgia for something we can never re-create. I feel like my teenage overprotective brother self again, and in that moment, I do what I would do as an act of kindness and affection to poor Rupa.

'Bundle,' I cry out, before running at the bed and jumping on to her body, careful to ensure my full weight doesn't wind her.

Noting my approach, and being older and wiser to my

moves, Rupa rolls on to her back and thrusts her knees in the air, so when I land, they press into my stomach.

I fall off her and slide off the bed.

She laughs.

I make a show of pulling at the covers and scrabbling on to the bed, where I lie next to her. I look up at her. Rupa looks at the door.

'Is he up?' she whispers.

I nod.

'Stop fighting,' Dad says, as if on cue, from the breakfast counter.

'Now,' I say. 'Would you like a cup of tea? Two sugars?'

'God no,' Rupa says. 'I drink coffee now. There's a cafetière in the cupboard.'

'My dude,' I say, springing off the bed, in search of delicious acrid caffeine.

At the door, I turn back to face her.

'Rups, are you okay?' I ask.

She nods, rubbing her eyes and yawning loudly.

'Yeah,' she says. 'Listen, forget what I told you yesterday. It's nothing, really.'

'I'm here if it becomes something.'

We meet for lunch. A rare occasion. We met once when she was at university and wanted me to approve of her then-boyfriend. I happen to be near where she works and text her, almost for the brownie points of an invite, to see if she spontaneously wants to meet for some food. I don't expect her to reply but she does, excitedly.

I suggest a dosa house.

She replies, *ur obsessed wit dat place.*

I sip at a mango lassi as I wait for her and scroll through her Facebook posts. It's the best way for us to stay in contact these days. Our appositely chaotic lives don't intersect very often.

When I hit 'one year ago', I notice a curious exchange between her and one of our other cousins.

Buried deep in a discussion of a photo of both of them looking amazing at a wedding is a conversation about white wine.

Rupa: hey, so I'm rlly getting into wine at the moment. I need yr advice.
Dolly: white wine? Wht abt archers n lemonade innit?
Rupa: I'm a sophisticated business woman now cuz. Plus my boss is alwys takin us out for dinner and he is rlly into his white wine. I need a crash course just to keep up.

I sit back in my chair and start to process the exchange.

'Hey idiot face,' I hear and look up.

It's Rupa, smiling.

She looks different in her work clothes. She doesn't look like her. She looks uncomfortable. Grey.

'What are you doing round here, then?' she asks.

'I had a meeting and I thought I'd see what you were up to,' I reply, turning my phone over so it's face down on the table. 'Plus, you know how much I love the lassis here.'

'True, you fat shit. What was the meeting about?'

'Oh, just some script they want me to write, literally because I'm Asian.'

'It's good to be wanted for something,' she replies, ordering a chai.

I hold up two fingers as if to say, one for me and the waiter nods at us both.

'It is good. But at the same time, I'm happy to be Asian. I just don't need to channel it to write a script. It's just innate in me. Anyway, you not that busy today?'

'What do you mean by that?' Rupa asks, curtly, looking around the room.

'It's just, you're not very good at being spontaneous innit. I'm surprised you could make it out.'

'My older brother asks me for lunch? Of course I'm gonna come. It's the rare occasion you pay for anything. Because of your duty.'

'To my very well-paid sister. I'm the starving artist remember?'

'I do,' Rupa says.

She looks down at her hands. I notice her shoulders shake so I reach out to touch her on the arm, tell her it's okay. She's too far away and we don't have that kind of relationship. My hands suddenly feel big and heavy. I don't want to keep looking at her because that's the worst when you're crying, the pity look from people around you, who are helpless but can't help try and communicate their empathy through pursed eyebrows and sad eyes.

'What's your favourite fish?' I ask.

Rupa looks up.

'What?' she says, wiping her cheeks.

'Your favourite fish. Cos, you see, I quite like meaty tasting fish, like tuna, or red snapper. I don't really like the delicate ones like sea bass. Remember when we thought I was allergic to prawns but it turned out I just had two bad runs of prawns in a row? Do you remember? You went out first thing and got me that Lucozade to drink, and the Spider-Man comic I requested. Gotta replace those electrolytes. Gotta—'

'Stop,' she says. 'Just stop. I'm okay. Leave it, please?'

I can't. Something in me, either fraternal or patriarchal or just aggressive male thinking he can solve all of women's problems everywhere can't switch off the tap of enquiry. I feel this compulsion, rising up in me that wants my sister to tell me everything, so I can become angry for her.

'The white wine thing,' I say. 'That's from your boss isn't it?'

She nods.

Her chai arrives. She stirs sugar into it for a long time. I look at the buffet offerings on the other side of the restaurant and then back to my sister.

'Do you want me to change the subject?' I ask.

She looks up from her chai and at me. She goes to speak but stops, as if she's considering her words, trying to temper them to my reaction, maybe she doesn't need me to get angry on her behalf.

'Look, I never felt easy with him, okay? Ever. From the moment he got the job, he changed. He used to be an account manager like me. Then he headed up all the accounts managers, and he changed. None of us knew where we were with him. And he was the funniest with me, okay? Also, arranging meetings then cancelling them at the last minute, setting me impossible deadlines, demanding I work late on days when I had plans, taking credit for my work. All of it, just all the worst things you imagine from one of those managers where they don't do anything explicit to show you something tangible that they're bad. Just a sea of passive-aggressive things. And I wanted a good work–life balance. Every Friday we all went for lunch, and he always ordered white wine, very specific, all these questions he had. And I thought, if I had that thing with him, that bond, then maybe he wouldn't treat me so horribly. Maybe. So I took some lessons, joined a club, read blogs, drank a lot of white wine, just to be on a level with him.'

'Do you think he had a thing for you?'

'No. Whether or not he wants to fuck me, it's got nothing to do with whether he's attracted to me.'

I pause.

I realise I'm talking over my sister, so I smile and look at my chai and wait for her to talk.

'I'm sorry,' I whisper.

'It's fine, look,' Rupa says. 'How's the script stuff?'

'It's fine,' I tell her. 'We had a forty-five-minute-long debate earlier over whether a character would eat breakfast or think it was a pointless meal earlier so I . . . live a stupid, woefully stupid existence. Sometimes I feel like I'm treading water in a hot tub. I'm waiting for my life to start but it is oh-so-cosy.'

'You do lead a silly life. Here I am, deciding whether a banner ad for a hotel or for insurance would fit better with the keyword holiday, just wishing you took life seriously for a change.'

'You know you can always chat to me,' I say. 'I know she's not around any more, to be your confidante and consiglieri. And I know Dad's Dad. And I know I'm a dumb sitcom writer. But talk to me. I can be serious when you need me to be.'

'I just need you to not be outraged. I need you to listen.'

We're at Shruti's mehndi, a little drunk and Rupa tells me she has cigarettes in her bag. Would I like one?

There's a park behind Markand mama's house. We used to play in it when we'd spend summers with Ba. I used to go there to watch people play basketball, imagining myself, the short guy, throwing beautiful three-pointers from the top of the D, listening to Ice Cube on my Walkman, while Rupa sat with her friends under a nearby tree, discussing which of the bhangra muffins on the court they all fancied. It was always Sandeep. He was lanky and cocky and talented but he had the longest eyelashes and he was definitely going to study pharmacy one day.

The irony is, our cousin Shruti is marrying him on Sunday.

We're at her mehndi. And the memories of what we used to be like when we were a whole family seem like a fantasy novel now – a long, long time ago and somehow not quite real.

Rupa and I have never smoked cigarettes together. Whenever I saw her, as a teenager, smoking behind St George's Shopping Centre, she looked so uncomfortable, angry. Whenever she saw me smoking, with the bhangra heads, in front of Calamity Comics, brazen, because it was the route Bapuji took to the post office. I was brazen but smoked with the cigarette cupped into the palm of my hand, so it was disguised from the casual passer-by, in case of a rogue masi or mama driving past, and easily disposed of.

We sit on swings.

Though it's dark and the park is empty, we can hear strains of noise from a corner where some giggling teenagers are doing balloons. The occasional squeal of the canister filling the balloon with the laughing gas makes Rupa and me flinch.

We smoke in silence, looking at our feet.

The thick rustle of the sequins on Rupa's dupatta jangle with her back-and-forth motion.

'I don't want to talk about it,' Rupa says quietly.

And we don't. We swing, we smoke, she taps me on the forearm when she's cold and ready to go back inside.

I meet Rupa outside her office on her last day there. She has amassed a collection of awards, bottles of white wine, a huge bouquet and other nick-nacks, involving her own mono-grammed dressing gown, and the blanket Mum used to wrap us all in to watch television.

I gesture to it as we pack it into the boot of my car.

'It felt comforting to keep my knees warm with it,' she says. 'That office was always cold.'

As we drive away, me navigating central London traffic with a clumsy lack of confidence, I ask where to next.

'Don't ask me. I don't know. I'm on gardening leave. I don't think I can look for a job yet. But don't ask me. I just don't want to talk about it.'

'I meant, am I taking you home? Or shall we go see if Dad's in?'

'I dunno, man,' she says. 'Just take me out of the city.'

As we straddle the thick traffic of buses, taxis and me-andering bicycles changing lanes almost arbitrarily, I apologise to my sister, my city, repeatedly.

'I've never been in a car with you,' she tells me as we hit the dual carriageway leading us towards our suburb.

'I'm terrible aren't I?' I say.

I only learned a year ago and still don't drive enough to have earned my 10,000 hours of expertise.

'Yeah, you're pretty terrible. I'm quite scared for my life.'

'Sorry.'

We listen to some Hindi songs Rupa made me as a driving mixtape when I passed. It's sat unlistened-to in the glove compartment all this time. She sings along. Occasionally I join her for a chorus, singing robotically so I can concentrate.

'You know,' she tells me. 'That time you had your wrist broken by that officer, the one who called you a jihadi, I thought you were making it up.'

'What?'

'Not the broken wrist, or the policeman. Just the comment: him calling you a jihadi. At the time, I couldn't understand why you didn't just tell him you weren't Muslim. It frustrated me when you told Mum and Dad that wasn't the point. Mum got it immediately.'

'I miss her,' I tell her.

'I feel like I'm out of my depth without her to check things for me. Like, I didn't even think what was happening to me was anything like what you went through. I was in denial for ages.'

'You're out of there now.'

'But he's not. That's the thing that bothers me. He can do whatever he wants and they will just get rid of us to protect him.'

'I know. That's the institution.'

'Why didn't you fight back? Against the policeman?'

'Because I shouldn't have to,' I say.

'Ella stopped being my friend in primary school because her daddy told her I was a Paki. It's amazing what you start remembering when things like this happen. All the things you internalised because you had to be grateful or fit in or just get on with life, making money, stuff like that.'

'It doesn't matter how long you've been fighting for, just that you do.'

'I didn't say I was doing anything,' she says. 'Can you pull over? I think I'm going to be sick.'

I pull up in a lay-by on the A40, just before our exit. Rupa gets out of the car and walks to the back. I put the hazard lights on and wait.

I hear the boot open and swing round in my seat. Rupa is rummaging around in her things.

I get out of the car.

The speed with which traffic passes us makes me feel unsteady for a second. I join her at the trunk.

She has lifted three bottles of white wine out and placed them on the pavement. She finds the fourth, and places it next to the others.

'Get rid of them,' she says, breathing lightly and anxiously. 'I can't look at them.'

She places her hands on her knees and hunches over, spitting on to the floor.

I look at the bottles.

She shouts. 'Get them away from me. Get that bastard's wine away from me. Get it away from me.'

I walk over to the pavement and pick the bottles up, one by one. I look at my sister. In that second, she looks so grown up, almost like our mum.

'Thank you,' she stammers, as I walk away from her. The bottles are heavy but soon they will be gone.

Mania

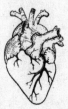

From Ancient Greek

man- crazy

From the term manic; a love that is possessive and obsessive; a frenzied love.

Mania is a love that is entirely devoid of rational thinking. It's obsessive and single-minded, addictive and turbulent, leaving no room for question or reflection. Often it's more about the person doing the loving, rather than the object of their affections.

Magdala, Who Slips Sometimes

Donal Ryan

Sometimes I think I'd love to be a prostitute. But only for impotent men. Or men with no tackle at all. That way I could use the thing that I have, that certain way, to make them feel manly and big without having them all the time trying to get inside of me. I made a promise to him years ago that I'd let no one else ever do that. And I don't think he's ever broken his promise to me.

I fell in love with him at his brother's funeral. The whole of fifth and sixth year was asked to go, in uniform, because his brother had gone to our school and was very loved by all accounts. He had his two hands clasped together between sympathisers and he was leaning a tiny bit forward towards his brother's coffin and the top button of his shirt was open above his tie. The redness of his cheeks was shocking against the whiteness of the rest of him. He was sixteen and I was nearly. His hair was jet black and longish and a curling strand of it was stuck to his cheek. He looked so beautiful, and so heroic in his grief, that I nearly took a weakness looking at him. I wanted so much to put my hand on his cheek and lift that strand of hair away from his face and to tuck it in behind his ear and to kiss him on the cheek where it had been that the need was all of a sudden like an aching pain inside in the centre of me. All through the rosary I looked at him, and ached, and all along the queue to sympathise I looked at him. I hardly remember the rest of the mourners, what way they were or how they looked, though I must have shook hands with every one of them because I always do. I don't remember how his brother looked laid out because I didn't look, because

63

I never do, but some of the girls said after they could see the mark of the rope on his neck.

I met him at the cannery arch weeks later, and I was wearing a cut-off denim mini and a tiny white belly top. I was shameless those days, I was full of joy and lightness. I didn't know anything of the heavy dread that settles itself on every life eventually. He kept looking at me that day, and everywhere I went he'd follow, and the whole crowd of us walked the towpath from Fogarty's field to the viaduct and back, and he stopped to try and light a fag but the wind off the river wouldn't let him and I knew in my heart and soul what he was really doing, and I told my friend Ruth to go on ahead and I hung back waiting, walking slow and watching the ground before my feet, and about half the way back I felt him behind me and I turned around and he said not a word but kissed me straight on my lips, hard at the start so it hurt, then softer, and he made a sighing noise like he was feeling relief to be kissing me, like something was lifted from him in that moment, and I truly thought my heart would burst. I had my runners in my hand because I'd been walking barefoot on the cool grass verge and I dropped them so I could put my arms around him properly and he took that to mean I was game, and I was.

We always were able to communicate like that. No words were needed. And I'm an awful talker, I go on and on, I love talking. I'm interested in things. Pottery and poetry are my two things now at the moment. It's no coincidence they're spelled nearly the same. They give me the same feeling. I love the classes in the Tech on Thursday evenings; your one that gives them is lovely. She has a really posh accent but still she's very down to earth. She has no grand notions I don't think. I love when she puts her hands over mine on the spinning clay. I feel a real connection with her, even though I can hardly pronounce her name.

I went to a few poetry readings in town this winter, in the

library and the new café. The library had a man from Mayo down, a big tall chap, gorgeous, with black hair. He read some of his poems and I bought the whole book of them afterwards and he signed it for me. He was really careful about the inscription. He wrote my name really slowly and deliberately, and then he said my name, and smiled and looked straight into my eyes and shook my hand as he gave me the book. I told Robert about him and he went mad. I got a shock even though I should have known it would happen. What was so good about him, he wanted to know. What's so good about writing fucking poems? I couldn't explain, and so I said nothing. I just sat still and waited. I secretly love when he's jealous like that.

I never had a right to him but then again I never claimed to. We were together unbroken from the day on the towpath until the end of the next year when he had to go to a prize-giving dinner dance with his hurling team and he took one of the posh girls. Ursula Fox. That was the most terrible day of my life, when he told me he was doing that. He told me he had to, he had no choice, his parents had him told. Nothing that came after ever felt as bad as that. Every do he had to go to after that, even his debs, maybe especially his debs, he took one or other of the posh girls. They'd be fighting over him, and Ursula Fox would be crying or crowing around school depending on whether she was being dropped or being brought. He had his pick, and they were all the one to him, I think, they were all on the approved list and they all looked kind of the same. None of them were shaped like me. There's a word for what I became: inured. It's a horrible word. No one should ever have to become inured. But the world isn't perfect, and it's too huge a place to be shaped to the will or want of one person.

I wouldn't talk to him for weeks and weeks after the dinner dance. He kept writing me letters, saying he was sorry, he couldn't live without me, please would I please please take him back, he couldn't breathe, his world was at an end. Please, Maggie, my Mag, my love. My mother asked who all the letters were from, and I told her Robert, and she said You'll have to forget about Robert, and I told her to go and get lost and to stay out of my business. I regretted it then straight away, seeing the pain on her face. Who's Robert? my father said from the corner beside the stove and we both told him at the exact same time to shut up. Then we laughed and she said Oh, my little girl, and she shook her head. My mother knew me inside out. After that first time a cold understanding grew between us that he'd give it a couple of weeks before calling to take me for a walk as far as the cannery arch or the old fisherman's cottage on the towpath, and neither one of us would mention the do he'd been to nor the girl that was brought to it nor his reasons for doing what he did because I knew, and what was the point in saying things aloud that are obvious and known?

I have a diorama made of our life together. It's laid on painted boards and set across four trestle tables and takes up most of the spare room. All the things we did are in it, all the highlights, arranged around a sculpture I made from hard clay, not the pottery clay, of the two of us. The sculpture isn't great because I'm still trying to perfect it, to get his face just right, the straight line of his jaw, and the way it curves, the way it resolves, so perfectly, so just right. Did Quattrocento finger fashion it? a poet somewhere asked, one of the really famous ones but I can't remember now which or in what poem, but he asked it about something or someone so beautiful that it or they must have been shaped by a master sculptor, a person with skill beyond the divine, who could make something sublime and perfect and I always think of that line when I see his face.

If you saw him in his wedding suit that day. He was never as handsome before or since I don't think, so easy with his own beauty. I was never as proud of him, and my heart was never as pierced. I know I said nothing was as bad as the first time with the dinner dance but I suppose when everything's said and done and the final reckoning is in, that'll be the worst day. Ursula Fox lost a pile of weight for her wedding, and she hadn't much to lose to begin with. She looked like a fart would blow her away. She looked like a person from a concentration camp. All bones and pointy edges, haggy and bent.

We don't always go to bed. We've known each other a long time now. Sometimes I tell him I don't feel like it but we end up doing it anyway. Sometimes he'll have an idea he got somewhere, from a film or a book or something, and he'll want to try it. I always know when he has an idea like that: he'll have a certain look, a half-smile, and he'll be looking me up and down before he talks, and he'll always start with, Now don't say no straight away. And sometimes his idea is good and sometimes not.

The diorama has a mock-up of the entrance to the Ailwee caves, and the two of us standing in it holding hands. And I got a dinky model of the exact car he had that day: his mother's BMW; and I got the right colour and everything because there's no point in doing a diorama unless it's accurate to real life and fully correct. Otherwise it's just toys for children to play with. And I have the towpath done with earth and small stones and tufts of plastic grass and the river is half a small pipe running along the edge, glued to the tableside the way it has the same position relative to the ground as in real life. I insist on the scale being the same across all the parts of the diorama: one to seventy-two. I have a model of the cinema made from cardboard and plywood and clay and the details of the frontage and the roof and the posters are all exactly perfect. The posters are all of the films we went to see the three times we went to the pictures. I googled them and reduced them and got them scanned and lasered onto tiny plastic boards the way they do it onto buns and cakes in bakeries for birthdays and all sorts of celebrations. He never had much

money that time we were of an age and able to go to the
cinema together; his parents were fierce tight with it. Posharses
that have plenty are always as tight as ducks' arses, my father
always said. That's how they have it.

The diorama has the old handball alley where we did it
first and I bled and he looked sorry and worried and he said
he should have spared up and got us a hotel room, or we at
least should have waited until someone had a free house and
a bedroom we could use, and he kind of nearly ended up
blaming me, but I brought him around again and we did it
again the next day and then we had the knack of it after that
and it was always easy, nearly. I have the faded lines on the
ground and walls the very same as they are in real life, and
the tiny entrance with the broken door hanging from the
hinges, and a tiny figure in a red-and-black checked shirt
crouched down beneath the ash tree at the bend of the road
that's meant to be his friend Donagh keeping guard for us. I
make the figures out of plasticine for everyone else and out
of proper modelling clay for him and me. I have a word for
the likes of Donagh, and his other friends, and even my friend
Ruth who was always there from the first days when I was
queen bee until the awful days when he went with those others
and we fell out over it when I got back with him, and even
my parents and his parents and even Ursula Fox and even his
son and daughter, and the whole world, actually, truth be told:
Peripheral. They're the Peripheral People. They're only on the
periphery of our shared existence, tiny moons orbiting our
planet, so small they couldn't even cause a ripple in our tran-
quil sea. You see how poetic I've gotten. I even wrote a poem
of my own a while back.

I said to my mother once, Why did you name me after a
prostitute? She went mad. What do you mean? she said, What
in the name of God do you mean? Magdala. After Mary
Magdalene, I said. The reformed prostitute. My mother took
her Bible from beside the breadbin and she slammed it on the

table with all her strength and she said, really slowly, Show me . . . in there . . . where it says . . . she was a *prostitute*. And I searched and searched the Gospels and I found nothing; not once, anywhere, does it say in the Bible that Mary Magdalene, Mary of the town of Magdala, was a prostitute. Only that she was devoted to her Christ, was His handmaiden and faithful servant and friend, foremost among His disciples, and she watched Him die and she came to His tomb and she beheld His risen self. My mother came back to herself and she said, I gave you that name that you may be faithful and true, that you may know there's salvation to be found in love. But I wonder sometimes do you cleave too hard to it, to the living out of that name.

There's a way you can live this life and not die. You have to be careful about things. It's hard to explain in words. I swam once in the water of a sheltered bay in the Aegean Sea. In the year I left him and went travelling, with all my credit union savings and a fair whack of my mother's. She was so happy the day I left, she covered my face with kisses as the bus pulled up and she kept saying Good girl, good girl, you're away now, you're away, go live your life, my lovely girl. And though she hugged me tight the day I arrived back I could see as much sorrow as love in her eyes. Anyway, I swam out a ways past the marker buoys and there was a gentle swell and the sun-dappled water was warm as mud, and I threaded water a while and the shore seemed distant and the sides of the bay had fallen away and I was on the edge of open sea and I emptied my lungs of air and tried to see could I let myself be carried away quietly from this world – all of a sudden that compulsion came on me, that quiet impulse to die – and I realised I couldn't sink. Even when I held myself perfectly still the water carried me, like it was embracing me, holding me, and bringing me gently back to shore. The salt in the water in some parts of the Aegean, the sheltered parts especially, those parts not washed by violent tides, makes it dense, more dense than a human body, even, so I was like a cube of ice in a glass of coke. But that's the way I feel about my whole life now. There's no point in trying to direct things, to be the master of myself. Better altogether to be carried by the swell, face turned up to the sun and the sky and the eyes of God.

I was the talk of the town for a long time. After his wedding it was months and months before he called to me and when he did my mother ran him. Then she had her stroke and wasn't able to muster herself for the fight and she slipped away on me one warm evening in May, with only a sigh. Robert shook hands with me and gave me a kiss on the cheek in the funeral home, the very same as I had done for him all the years before when we were in school. And he even called in on his way home from the bright city from his office without texting ahead one evening the following week, and he sat by the stove with my father awhile and they chatted low and serious, and I heard my father saying Thanks, son. You're very good to call. We're lonesome after her all right. What's this your first name is again? I was the talk of the town for sure. But my mother said one time, There's neither glory nor shame in being the talk of this town, because this isn't much of a town. A thing becomes old news very quick, anyway, and unless it changes into something else it stops being talked about, and starts to be passed around in the currency of nods and winks and elbows instead of words.

Every part of him bar his backbone is perfect. He was led along a path and made no move to deviate himself from it. The very same as he used to lead me by the hand along the towpath by the river to the long grass at the side of the swimming hole to lie down with him beneath the sun and he'd cover me in kisses head to toe. He told me once what his house was like after his brother did away with himself. The way it hardened and took on sharp corners and how there was suddenly creaks everywhere and places you couldn't step, and all of a sudden had to be negotiated like a swamp full of hidden creatures with razor teeth. How none of them could any longer be easy or free. How he and his sister had to give their whole evenings long to homework and studying and he had only me and hurling training as relief from it, and his father was never in from the land and the horses until late and his mother's mouth turned down at the corners and never changed from that shape again. It's no wonder when you think about it he was afraid to ever go against them. It's no wonder, he couldn't bear to cost them any more pain. But still, wouldn't you think they'd have left their second son to find his joy after the hard lesson of their first? I'm his joy, his secret space, his relief and his salvation; he owns me and I him, and that's the why of it and the holy all of it.

I go into the city once a fortnight to the Vincent de Pauls. I give a hand in the soup kitchen and on the meals-on-wheels runs. There's a man about my own age who volunteers as well, a kind of a strange fish, but pleasant and obliging all the same. He looks more homeless than the customers some days, straggled and streelish and thrown together. There's never a bad smell off of him, though. He asked me once would I go to see a play with him. His friend wrote it, he said, and his chest puffed out a bit in vicarious pride. I said I couldn't and he just nodded exaggeratedly, though not in a smart or cynical way, and he didn't wait for a reason or press the issue. He just deflated himself and assumed his customary shape and shuffled sideways back along the serving counter with his ladle dripping stew along the floor. He calls to me at home here now and then. He knocks in and says he was just passing though I don't know where he could be passing to because he lives in the city and there's nothing out here; we're on the road to no place except back to the same road that brings you here. He sits in Daddy's old chair and he smokes roll-ups non-stop and there's a kind of a curve to him as he sits there, a nervous hunch, a shape of thwarted expectation. He culti-vates a little pointy beard. He showed me some of his poetry but it's terrible stuff. Not within an ass's roar of my man from Mayo. Why must all humans be measured and matched? Every poet must be held against my Mayo man, and every man must be held against my Robert.

I slip sometimes. I talk to Mammy and Daddy across the dark, forgetting in a moment's reverie that they're gone. I find myself at the kitchen table, hands clasped together before me and my eyes closed. I was never given to prayer but anyone looking in from the street window would think that's what I was doing. The truth is I give some days to living in memories. I have every detail stored of the best of our days, and I can call them up from the back of my mind at will. I can put all the details together the exact way they were in real life. Like my dioramas they're true to life in every tiny way. The days he used to hold my hand along the street. The days he kissed me in the corridor at school and everyone knew he was mine and I was his and there was no argument about it from anyone and his friends smirked and gurned like young lads do and the posh girls wrinkled up their little noses in disgust but I was happy beyond happiness, beyond reason; the whole universe exploded into being and existed those billions of years for me and him and us alone to be together there and then.

I slip sometimes. I put my hand on his son's shoulder in SuperValu one day, and I said Hello, Tiernan. And he swung around and looked up into my face expectantly, and his eyes were so like his father's it knocked the breath from me. There was a smear of something on his cheek and I wiped it away with the side of my thumb and I cupped his little chin in my hand for a minute and I said, Oh, Robert, you were such a lovely child, and his little face wrinkled in wonder and he said, That's my daddy's name. And I backed away from him softly before his mother turned around from the meat counter where she was reading Dinny Gleeson the riot act over fatty bits in ribeye steaks and pushing her expensive-looking buggy in and out from her too fast for the age of the little baby girl inside in it, and Dinny was telling her there was meant to be fatty bits in them, she needed to buy fillets if she didn't want fat.

I'm well on the road to forty now. It doesn't seem real. Seasons melt together and evaporate away. Sometimes I see Mammy and Daddy in the kitchen, looking into a playpen and making all sorts of noises and songs, and a baby just after learning to crawl and to sit up steady, inside in his little world of teddies and toys and teething rings, looking back out at them, smiling gummily up at them, his bare legs splayed out and his chubby knees, raising his little arms to be lifted out, and Daddy reaching straight away in for him and Mammy saying, Will you leave him inside in it, Noel, for the love of God, you've him pure spoilt going around with him above in your arms, his bones won't develop that way and he'll never sit still for Maggie the way you have him ruined; and I can see that and hear it exactly as if it was real, as if they were all three made of flesh and bone and not swirling dust that catches light a certain way as it streams in through the slats of the blinds to cross the empty space.

He can't help himself and nor can I, and the world can't help but to be the way it is. That notion I once had when I skipped and laughed through all my days and wore skirts so short that old men's ears turned purple and their faces boiled, and had the hand and the heart of my man for all to see, that the universe was fashioned just for us, that we were the most perfect things in all creation, only lasted a short while, a school term and a bit, and one summer holidays. A car drew alongside us one lunchtime near the chipper, and a man with a jowly face and a pink baldy head looked up at Robert and then at me and back at Robert and said only this: What the fuck are you doing with that one? Cop the fuck on to yourself and stop making a show of your mother and father after all they've been through. And he drove off with his wheels spinning as though even his big swanky car was in a temper of disgust, and he swung around the monument in the square and he drove back towards us again and he raised a warning finger at Robert as he passed, and his mouth was twisted and pursed, and all the time Robert had just stood still, with his can of orange half drank in his hand, and not a word did he say and nor did I, but the universe rearranged itself in those moments, and all the planets and the stars were once more properly aligned, and I resumed my proper place as a speck, a fraction of nothingness far, far from its centre.

I slip sometimes. I sat last week behind Ursula Fox's mother at an open meeting of the tidy towns committee. I sat and listened for a word of Rob or anything to tell me anything about his life. He doesn't talk to me about anything like that, the happenings within the four walls of his house, the life he carries on behind the high gates, behind the intercom and camera. He spends some evenings here fully in silence, and I stand behind him and stroke his hair and plant kisses on the top of his head and on the side of his face, and sometimes a tear rolls down along his cheek and follows the curve of his jaw to his chin and it hangs there a moment before it drops, or before I gather it in my fingers and hold my fingers to my lips to taste its salty sweetness on my tongue.

I sat behind Ursula Fox's mother and I heard her saying to the witchy-looking woman beside her that she was terribly worried, that she thought it was terribly irresponsible of them to have allowed it to happen, that Ursula was far too frail for a late pregnancy, and a boy and girl was just lovely, why couldn't they have been satisfied at that? I slip sometimes, and bang off people; I'm clumsy that way when I get a shock. My legs give way a little and I have to steady myself and gather myself, and I fell against the back of Mrs Fox's chair as I rose from mine, and I gave her a nasty dig of my elbow into the back of her coiffured fucking blue-rinsed head, and I told her I was sorry, and I was.

He sits here some evenings at the table and he twines his fingers into mine and I watch the lines that zigzag from the corners of his eyes across his temples and the touch of grey that's starting in his hair, and I feel the terrible weight of his longing and his regret, that he forsook me for others, that he forsook himself, and I tell him truthfully that I don't mind, I don't mind, there was nothing else that could be done, and he closes his eyes against his tears, and I close mine as well, and I imagine that we're lying in the long grass by the bend of the river, watching the birds and the westering sun.

I slip sometimes and let myself be interrupted by a sudden gust of wind around the eaves or a rumbling creamery lorry that shakes the window glass and the crockery in the cupboard as it passes along the street outside or a door slammed hard somewhere along the terrace and he crumbles like dry clay beneath my fingers and he fades to swirling dust that catches light a certain way as it streams in through the slats of the blinds to cross the empty space.

I slip sometimes and go to bed with streelish men bedraggled by their loneliness, with hangdog eyes and pointed beards, who try and try to marshal words to beauty and always fail. I slip sometimes and cry out Robert's name as they enter and my echo lands on empty sheets and I close my eyes and plead with fate to allow their seed to take.

I slip sometimes and drive my car along the golf links road and past the lines of poplar trees and park below the rise that leads to the high gates of his house, where he lives a life that I can't see, and I sit there with my window open and I listen to the gentle sounds of the stream and the breeze and the rustling grass and I hear his whispered promise that he'll love me all his days.

I slip sometimes and fall from reason's grace as I wait to feel the life within me stir, a boy I'm sure, with jet-black hair and deep-blue eyes, like his real father, who'll point and sing and smile up at the swirling dust that catches light a certain way as it streams in through the slats of the blinds to cross the empty space.

Storge

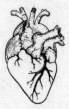

From Ancient Greek

stor- spread; ge- earth

Love for family; instinctive affection; natural attachment, especially to a child.

Though storge is similar to agape, it is reserved especially for familial bonds, and more particularly for the bond between parent and child (especially maternal).

Codas

Carys Bray

When Big Kev called to say Dad had gone down like a sack of potatoes during the Under-15s match, Louise thought it was his heart. He was at that age. Things were beginning to wear thin: his knee cartilage and hair, his jokes.

'He's fine,' Big Kev insisted. 'Absolutely fine. But I think you should come back.'

She'd already spent ninety minutes standing on the touch-line at Buckley Hill watching the Under-14s, stomping her wellied feet and shivering while Dad directed play with expansive arm gestures and Big Kev yelled, 'Under-14s? You're playing like Under-4s – that was an open goal!'

Max had scored a hat-trick. Of course she was pleased, but there should, she felt, be a rule in junior football that demanded the early conclusion of a match once the goal difference was more than ten. At the very least there should be a decibel cap on celebrations. Big Kev and some of the parents never knew when to give it a rest, cheering the twelfth goal like the first, oblivious to the growing stiffness of the opposition goalkeeper; every whoop, every shout of *get in* another slap on his poor, cold-reddened cheeks.

Earlier, before the match, she'd tucked a piece of gammon into the slow cooker, and now, as she stood, phone in hand, she was aware of the salt and smoke aroma trickling into the lounge, camouflaging the whiff of an unwashed Max who was deep in the throes of a Fifa tournament, Xbox controller clasped in rigid, concentrating hands.

'I've got to go back to Buckley Hill.'

'*Un-lucky*,' Max said, over his shoulder. It was his latest catchphrase, borrowed from a YouTube video featuring a Liverpool player, and uttered with all the sincerity of a game show host.

'Grandad's tripped over.'

'You could go off-roading on that pitch, it's well bumpy,' he replied, eyes fixed firmly on the television screen. 'Is he all right?'

'Kev says he's fine, but I'm going to make sure. Don't forget to shower,' she called as she left.

The Sunday roads were quiet. And Louise, who was at the age of unwelcome surprises, entertained her worst thoughts. Dad was active, a non-smoker, but she didn't know whether he'd ever had his cholesterol or blood pressure checked. Probably not. Had there been signs, she wondered: irregularities, skipped beats, a worn wire weakening the spark of his heart?

Big Kev was waiting in the car park when she arrived back at Buckley Hill. He was wearing his Assistant Manager hoodie, the one he'd had printed specially. Louise had known him her whole life. Even in his sixties, there was still something of the playground about him: she gave him a wide berth at matches because he had a tendency to call her Skip-to-the-Lou, and if he ever caught her yawning on the touchline, he'd lean over and stick his finger in her mouth. He and Dad used to play amateur football together until finally, after sustaining a series of injuries in the Over-40s league, they had to be content with doing their coaching badges and a spot of recreational, walking football on the side. At sixty-nine Dad was the oldest coach at the club and the only one to oversee two teams. He had been coaching the Under-14s – Max's team – and the older Under-15s for almost a decade.

Kev opened the driver's door before she'd had a chance to kill the engine and escorted her across the network of pitches, unnecessarily leading the way with an orchestrating arm.

Dad was sitting on someone's fold-up chair – he certainly didn't own such a thing – elbows on his knees, head resting in his hands. It was still cold, the hard bright sun no more than a speck in the pewter sky, but he was wearing shorts, the hair on his legs a grey mat over purpling skin.

'The Gaffer wiped out.' Kev placed a meaty paw on Dad's shoulder. 'I thought it was his knee. He wasn't running, though, were you, mate? I wouldn't let him, honest. It was just a fast walk, you wouldn't even call it a jog. But he hit the deck, somehow. Got up right away, but he felt funny.' He looked to Dad for corroboration. 'You feel funny, don't you? Phil?'

The Under-15s game continued apace. Dad didn't speak, he just tilted his head, as if there was water in one of his ears and by dislodging it he might restore himself.

'Fell faint,' Dad said as Louise clasped his arm and helped him to his feet

'You felt faint?'

'Yes.'

'Or you were faint, and then you fell?'

'Yes.'

'I'm going to take you to the hospital, just to make sure. We'll come back for your car later.'

He nodded, and Louise knew she was doing the right thing because he'd given in so easily.

As she drove, she took sidelong glances at him, waiting for him to comment on the state of the car: the thicket of used parking tickets, the cluster of empty chocolate wrappers. He kept drawing breath, as if he was preparing to dive into something – conversation, water, an argument – and then he sat open-mouthed, poised to speak yet empty of words. Bewilderment followed: a short laugh, a shake of his head, another prefatory breath, and more silence.

Not his heart, she thought. And, driving down the dual carriageway to the hospital, she was suddenly blasé about hearts. They were just plumbing, she decided. Appliances, with replaceable pipes, ducts and vents. People were still themselves after grafts and bypasses and pacemakers. But – she glanced again at the open socket of Dad's mouth – the brain was mysterious, certainly to her. Diagrams of brains in Max's biology textbook reminded her of butchers' silhouettes of cows; dotted lines scoring the various cuts of meat: chuck, brisket, shank. The division of the brain looked similar: visual, motor, auditory, each area represented in a different pastel shade, notwithstanding the reality; the grey squiggle of hairpin bends that surely made it impossible to know exactly where one function ended and another began.

His brain, then. There was an acronym she should remember. She was unsure if it started with 'S' for 'smile' or 'M' for 'mouth'. Maybe 'F' for 'face' – she couldn't think. And without that first letter, how was she to work out the word itself and the other symptoms?

'Can you smile?' she asked, while stopped at traffic lights.

He could, and his face seemed level. But there was a vagueness in his expression, all his keenness wiped out like fog off a window.

'What was the score when we left, Dad?'

He looked up at himself in the mirrored sun visor, as if hoping to see the answer in his open mouth.

'How about before half time?'

He couldn't say, didn't appear to know.

'Max's game, earlier, do you remember that score?'

It was hard to conceive that he didn't. He made notes after every match and he and Max frequently discussed games from years ago, recalling not just scorelines, but memorable fouls and classic mistakes by referees – these, of course, were innumerable. She, on the other hand, barely remembered a single detail. This, despite spending the Saturday mornings of her childhood standing behind the touchline supporting Dad, and the afternoons sitting beside him on the sofa in front of

Grandstand: Des Lynam's moustache, Zola Budd running barefoot and Torvill and Dean's Bolero – Louise remembered these things. She remembered Mum mowing the hoover through the lounge during the Olympic 100m final and the Grand National. She remembered the family holiday to Germany in 1988 that had turned out to be a trip to the European Football Championships where England lost every one of their group matches. And she remembered pestering for piano lessons, and Dad's injunction that it might be better to learn something she could play in an orchestra; a team instrument.

The space outside Accident and Emergency was reserved for ambulances. Louise stopped on the double yellow lines just around the corner. She turned the hazard lights on, hurried to the passenger side of the car and opened the door.

'Can you undo your seat belt?'

'Yes,' he said.

'All right.' She gave him a moment. 'Can you do it now?'

'Yes.'

'Come on, then. The button, it's just there, Dad . . . Can you lift your right hand? High, so I can see it. Dad?'

'Yes.'

But he didn't. It was as if he was operating in Safe Mode; concentrating on core processes, loading up as few programmes as possible. She reached into the car and unfastened the belt herself. Then she ran back around the corner, through the automatic doors and into the Accident and Emergency waiting area. At the back of the room were two glass windows, one labelled Reception, the other Triage, with a PLEASE DO NOT DISTURB sign beneath. She knocked on that window, before opening the door beside it to disturb a pair of nurses.

'I think my dad's having . . .' She didn't want to say the word in case it conjured the thing. Stupid, she knew. And she didn't want to be dismissed as hysterical in the event that it was nothing, a funny five minutes, an extended senior moment. But if it was serious, her reticence would be a reproach. 'I think,' she began again, 'I think my Dad's having a stroke and I can't get him out of my car.'

'I'll get a chair,' one of them said. But she didn't rush. No one rushed. It wasn't like it was on the television.

Louise lingered beside PLEASE DO NOT DISTURB, aware that everyone in the waiting room had heard and was watching: the old woman with a tea-towel pressed to her head; the ruddy-faced man with a hand held theatrically to his heart; the girl with the bandaged ankle who was on her phone stage-whispering, 'I was so pissed last night, I never felt it 'til I woke up this afternoon.'

The nurse emerged with the wheelchair and Louise led her outside and around the corner where the car hugged the kerb, lights flashing.

'Hello, shall we get you out of the car, then? What's his name?'

'Phil.'

'Can you get out of the car, Phil?'

'Yes.'

'Up you get then, Phil.'

'Yes.'

'How about now? I'm in a bit of a hurry.'

'I think we'll have to help him,' Louise said. 'I don't think he can . . .'

The nurse swivelled his legs so they were facing the pavement and tugged on his right arm. His hand, Louise noticed, was clenched. Once he'd managed to stand, he couldn't seem to sit. The nurse had to push on his shoulders until he folded in the middle and his behind made surprise contact with the seat of the chair.

'He was fine, earlier.' She walked alongside the nurse. 'He coaches football. He played for years. He does walking football now, it's this new thing for older . . . he has to be careful, he's got a dodgy knee. He's very active, though. He fell. I don't know why.' She was blabbing. Dad's silence wasn't helping, if anything it felt like he was egging her on. The automatic doors to A&E wooshed open. 'I'll just move the car,' she said. 'I'll be straight back.'

On her return she ignored the PLEASE DO NOT DISTURB sign for the second time and entered the triage room.

'. . . you feeling poorly, Phil?'

'Yes.'

'And you had a fall, earlier?'

'Yes.'

'Does your head hurt?'

'Yes.'

'Did you bang it when you fell?'

'Yes.'

'I don't think he did. His friend didn't mention it. I think he's just saying yes to everything. Ask him where he lives or how old he is.'

'How old are you, Phil?'

Dad took a breath and presented the nurse with the empty *oh* of his mouth.

'Can you answer that question for me please, Phil?'

'Yes.'

'Good, so how old are you?'

Dad shook his head.

'See?' Louise said, frightened.

When they wheeled him away for a CT scan she went outside and called David.

'I'm at the hospital with Dad,' she said, after the beep – he never answered when her number came up. 'I think I might be a while. Could you have Max tonight? The slow cooker's on. Eat the gammon, if you like. Can you text and let me know you've got this? I've got a little bit of signal in A&E. Oh, and make him have a shower, will you?'

While she was there she texted Max and Big Kev before heading indoors where she bought a cup of burnt coffee and waited.

He looked like he'd been poured into the bed when they wheeled him back into the curtained cubicle. She tucked the thin blanket around him, leaving his arms out before changing her mind and covering them up. She tried sitting on the hard plastic chair, but it was low and she couldn't see him properly so she stood again, and waited. Finally, one of the doctors returned.

'The scan shows that there's been some bleeding between Phil's brain and the tissue covering it,' she explained. 'He's going to need an operation. Probably this evening, we're just making some calls.'

Louise went outside again. It was already mid-afternoon and the light was beginning to fade. She checked her phone. There was a message from David: *OK*. Moments later she intercepted Big Kev, a cosy crime novel in one hand and a tube of BBQ Pringles in the other; in it for the long haul, he said. She sent him away; Dad was asleep, although what she labelled sleep was beginning to more closely resemble unconsciousness. And anyway, the thought of Kev loitering in Accident and Emergency, poised to tackle her if she slipped outside, was too much.

It was like a mining accident, she decided, back in the cubicle. There had been a collapse. And yes, Dad was trapped, but perhaps he had found an air pocket in one of the twists of brain tissue, and when the flood of blood receded he would emerge, gasping and intact, ready to resume his role as parent and well-intentioned haranguer. Only the previous night he'd phoned to check whether she'd made any effort to meet someone. And she had sighed and settled back on the sofa, phone tucked between chin and shoulder, ready to reiterate that using her free time to watch television and browse the internet was not the abnegation he believed it to be.

'I know the more I mention this, the less likely you are to do it,' he said. 'But if *I* don't bring it up, who will?'

'What about *you*?' she tried, but she couldn't outlast him in the silence that followed, eventually breaking it with her go-to excuse: 'I don't know what to put on a profile.'

'I know, love. That's why I've come up with some suggestions.'

'Oh. You really didn't have to—'

'How about this?' He cleared his throat and she heard the crackle of paper. '*Liverpool fan, tired of walking alone. Looking for goalkeeper, defender, midfielder or striker who plays fair and doesn't need to be subbed or sent off.*'

She laughed. 'It makes me sound a bit desperate. The bit about goalie, striker, midfielder – it sounds like anyone'll do.'

'All right. What about this one? *Reds supporter, tired of walking alone* – it's good that bit, so I've kept it – *seeks free transfer and long-term relationship with fellow football fan.*'

'The free transfer bit – it's like saying I'll grab anyone, even if he's on someone else's team. And I'm not sure about "reds supporter". You know I'm not bothered about football, not really.'

'Max is bothered. And we don't want an Evertonian in the family, do we? Anyway, I've got some others. Are you listening or are you watching TV?'

She grabbed the remote and pressed mute.

'This is a cheeky one,' he warned. '*Sign language expert, good with her hands, seeks gentleman for silent communication.*'

'Oh, God.' She laughed again. 'Firstly, I'm not an expert, I did that course years ago. And secondly, I *can't* say that.'

'This one, then. *Reds supporting piano teacher, hoping to be closely marked, pursued and eventually tackled by fellow educator.* No? I've got more; I wrote them on the back of an envelope yesterday, while I was waiting at the doctor's.'

'Oh Dad,' she'd said, not thinking to ask whether he was all right.

*

They took him away after she signed a form acknowledging that they may not bring him back. The daylight faded as she sat on the wall at the front of the hospital beside the smokers and signal hunters. She read about the operation on her phone; its conveniences and complications. They would insert a catheter just above his hip and snake it up his internal highways. There must be a map; a way of plotting his A and B roads, his contraflows and junctions. She found a model of the human blood vessels – they were beautiful, an efflorescent, spun-sugar tangle – and she zoomed in, attempting to trace her way from hip to brain. But it was like the maze puzzles in her childhood colouring books, there were false starts and dead ends and once she got past the neck, the vessels looked as fine as thread. When they reached the aneurysm they would pack its bulge with tiny platinum coils and perhaps insert a diversion device to scaffold the vessel wall. It all sounded so straightforward. Like repairing a pothole. Maybe she was wrong, and brains were mostly plumbing, too.

Louise trudged up and down the spine of the central corridor, long past the hunger that could be fixed with something from a vending machine. She wondered about the gammon. Had David and Max eaten it or was it sitting on a plate in the fridge, a soft, pink chunk of flesh wrapped in cling film? Her stomach clenched. The café and shop were closed and the welcome desk abandoned. The black windows echoed the night back at her. Time was twisting, the minutes expanding to accommodate hours. She returned to the relatives' room and read magazines from the previous year while intermittently checking her watch.

The surgery was followed by *getting him settled* and *making him comfortable* and then she was finally allowed to see him; mended, unblocked and surrounded by machines whose beeps droned *wait-and-see, wait-and-see*.

He slept. Once or twice he opened his eyes and looked at

her before closing them again. She held the bud of his right hand and unfurled his closed fingers, one, two, three, four; watching as they curled back over the crook of his thumb, tight with exhaustion, perhaps. She remembered sleeping like that when she was small, whorling her whole self into a knot.

The most persistent of the machines beeped an E or E flat. Once she had noticed it, the sound expanded until it percussed in her head like a triangle roll. Her teeth felt furry and her mouth tasted of coffee and empty stomach. It was clear that he was in no immediate danger and finally, mouth square with the effort of not yawning, she returned to the relatives' room for a nap. Although the chairs there were softer and bigger than those on the ward and in A&E, she couldn't find the right position for sleep; the wipeable plastic upholstery squeaked against the bum of her jeans every time she moved. She thought of Dad's car, still parked at Buckley Hill; she'd have to find a way to pick it up, preferably one that didn't involve asking David for help. She would need to cancel tomorrow's – no, today's piano lessons. And she would have to Skype Mum. Eventually, she settled, only to become attuned to her inside noises; she was plugged in and humming like a fridge.

It wasn't long before daylight jabbed the window and the sound of traffic barged past the glass. She heard trolley wheels scraping up and down the corridor. Voices, as staff arrived for work. And she decided to check on Dad one more time, then go home.

The connection was poor and Mum's voice echoed badly, ricocheting off her stone walls and tile floors. 'You're not expecting me to fly over?'

'No,' Louise said, although it would have been nice, if only for her sake.

'I feel bad, but you wouldn't expect me to . . . I mean, *you* wouldn't, for David, would you? Not in the circumstances.'

Louise experienced the unwelcome realisation that she would. Maybe, in time, her feelings would change. Mum and Dad had split up when Max was a baby. Dad and Kev were beginning to talk about doing their coaching badges when Mum announced that she had been looking forward to weekend breaks and regular holidays during retirement, and she would be taking them with someone else. There was no shouting. It seemed they'd run out of feelings. Afterwards, Dad quipped that, according to the rules, delaying play was not a sending-off offence. The gag was like a soft pedal, an attempt to dampen any reverberations.

'So it went well, the operation?'

'They said so.'

'I hope he gets better soon. Say that to him, if you like. Are *you* all right?'

'Yes.'

'And Max?' Mum peered into the screen, as if she might discover him.

'He's at school.'

'Oh. Of course. I'm sure your Dad will be fine, love. He'll be a terrible patient,' she warned as Roy stepped into the room in a pair of high-waisted slacks, holding a mug in each hand. 'He'll want spectators. Kev and the lads, standing around the bed, applauding his progress: "Good one, Phil!" *You* won't get a look-in.'

Louise smiled. Dad never made jokes about Mum, though he considered Roy, who had once described bridge as a sport, to be fair game.

'Well, we're off to watch a film at the British Society in a bit, so I'll love you and leave you. I can't remember how to . . . How do you? Roy, can you find the . . .'

Roy leaned across to help and the screen froze as the buttons of his dress shirt held on for dear life.

*

The words fell out of Dad's mouth, rough-hewn and lumpen. He told her his *earsight* and *searing* were fine. He made it to the toilet and back and then he needed a nap.

'The problem is,' he began when he woke.

She waited for him to expound on the problem, unsure whether she should ignore the loose end of the sentence or attempt to tie it for him.

'I feel cut in half,' he said, later. 'That,' he glanced down at his right arm, 'doesn't feel like me.'

If some connections had been blocked or temporarily diverted, the link between his thoughts and speech was newly wireless. In a very loud whisper he announced a preference for the *dark nurse*, the one with *fluffy arms*. He also registered his disgust with the man in the next bay who had *shat the bed*.

Louise shushed him. 'Kev's desperate to see you,' she said. 'And Andy from walking football sent a couple of texts to your phone, so I replied. He'd like to come, too. With . . . Mike? – I think he said Mike.'

'No.'

'Why?'

'Not yet.' He glanced down at his fastened fist.

'It'll be boring with just me coming. They think you'll be in for at least a week or two.'

'If it's boring, you don't . . .' he managed before the end of his sentence fell away.

'*I'm* not bored. I meant you; *you'll* be bored.'

She held his right hand and played his digits like keys: one, two, three, four, five; do, re, me, fa, so; hearing the notes in her head as she mimed the five-fingered piano songs she taught beginners: 'Jingle Bells', 'Oranges and Lemons', 'Ode to Joy', eventually lulling him back to sleep.

Instead of dropping Max home, David suggested a handover at the coffee shop and, afraid of appearing churlish, Louise agreed. He would offer to pay, she knew. And he would sit across the table, pretending an interest in everything she said. She hated to think of him going home and patting himself on the back for being civilised.

'I was reading about this bloke who could suddenly play the cello after being struck by lightning,' David said as he placed the tray on the table; he was always reading, his hobbies were solitary, no team sports for him. He passed Max his hot chocolate and Louise picked up her latte. 'Brain injuries can do that. Some people speak a different language after a burst aneurysm. Or they get an accent.'

Louise watched as Max's lips twitched; a staccato smile that acknowledged her discomfort and invited patience.

'There was a bloke who felt happy all the time. He lost the ability to feel sadness.' David's gaze flicked from her to his drink. He looked guilty. Their years together sat in the bank of his memory like a bad debt; earlier that afternoon the obligation had clearly driven him to Wikipedia, in search of something remotely comforting to say.

As David continued to describe the more unusual consequences of brain injuries, Louise studied him: bare forearms, sleeves rolled past his elbows, fingers clasping the sides of his mug rather than its handle, and she wanted to put him on, like an old jumper.

He paused and took a gulp of coffee before continuing. 'And there was a straight rugby player who woke up after a stroke to discover that he was actually a gay hairdresser. Anything can happen.'

It was an anecdote too far, even Max realised as much and planted his mug on the table top like a full stop.

After they'd eaten beans on toast, Max started his homework. Louise watched his bent head as she tidied the kitchen. The way his hair sprouted from the base of his skull in a straight line, like David's. Usually, she was in the front room at this time of day, sitting beside other people's children as they made excuses about practice and fudged their scales. Max had never been interested in learning to play music. Watching Dad coax him into football had made her glad to have been born at a time when no one expected girls to play. There had always been something elastic between the pair of them. Dad had called him 'Little Matey' until he was about eight. Then it was 'Mate', the same as Kev and Dad's other friends. Louise used to notice the unintentional deepening of Max's voice when they were together; the effort Max expended when carrying the match bag, stuffed full of spare balls, kit, shin pads and the first-aid kit. Now there was no need for an excavated voice, and Max, who was almost as tall as Dad, carried the bag on one shoulder, hands free to heft other equipment.

'I'm popping back to the hospital for a bit, Max.'

'I'll get my coat.'

'Maybe tomorrow.'

'*Un-lucky*,' he said, as he dropped his pen and pushed back the chair.

'He doesn't want any visitors. Just me.'

He froze for a moment before sitting back down, hard. 'Fine,' he said.

She took the back roads, and played Prokofiev's 'Suggestion Diabolique', the volume ratcheted up to twenty. The music was angry and indignant, bursting with spite. Losing David had been like a slow puncture – the last of the air was leaking out now; brackish and sour.

'I need to tell you something,' he had said, almost two years ago.

Nothing good had ever followed such an opener; Louise awaited the damage.

'I love you, but I'm not *in love* with you any more.'

Many years previously, before they had Max, when love was love and the partitioning of it was out of the question, they'd had hypothetical conversations – 'If you didn't love me any more, you'd tell me, wouldn't you?' – and although she had literally asked for it, she had wished, in that moment, that he would either shut up or lie.

How to sleep in the same bed as the man who is no longer in love with you, but says he will stay, *for now*? How to lie next to him? How to arrange your legs and arms so as not to accidentally touch him? Louise hadn't shared a bed with someone who didn't love her for years and was struck by the newness of it, until it dawned on her that she'd been doing it for some time, unwitting and oblivious; draping herself over him, lacing her legs with his, curling into his back in the small hours, one arm under her pillow, the other circling his belly – jet-packing, they called it. And it seemed different now, the past jet-packing; as if, while lying on his side, facing the bedroom door, he'd been imagining escape, and she had interrupted his fantasies of freedom by folding herself around him, the piggy on his back.

At first, she imagined there was something she could do: lose weight, be tidier, stay up with him on clear nights as he gazed through his telescope. She bestowed forgetful strokes and unwitting confidences. Eventually, she learned to rein herself in; until, words tucked into the pouch of her mouth, hands into the pockets of her trousers, she grew exhausted by the pretence of nonchalance and David moved out.

In the weeks that followed she rummaged through piles of sheet music and, while Max was at school, she played arrangements of Dido's 'Lament', Barber's 'Adagio for Strings', and Elgar's 'Enigma Variations' – the house sounded like Remembrance Sunday or a state funeral.

'But he loves you,' Dad had protested when she told him, seemingly more upset about the disintegration of her marriage than his own, though perhaps disquiet is more easily expressed by proxy. 'Love! *In*-love! What's the difference? What does he *mean*? Love is *love*.'

Later that evening, at the hospital, as she smoothed the sheet around a sleeping Dad, it occurred to her that he was probably the only person in the world who couldn't begin to imagine why David didn't love her any more.

Max balanced on his toes as he reached for the breakfast cereal and there it was, in his posture, the ballet. It still surprised her.

Months ago, having watched a programme about athletes learning to dance, he had announced his intention to do the same. She searched online and eventually found a beginners' class for teens. She wasn't to tell anyone. Not David or Dad, and especially not Big Kev. None of his mates at school were to know, either. He was changing fast, shoulders broadening, arms thickening, the soft chub of his cheeks narrowing, and while she missed his younger, open-book face, she felt a small spike of pleasure every time she remembered their secret.

She watched as he stepped to the fridge, feet pointed, shoulders back.

'What?' he said. '*What?*'

'Nothing,' she replied.

She loved him so much that she sometimes found herself bursting with unexpected hurts. That morning, it was the realisation that she would not be able to care for him when he was an old man; someone else would have to look after him, someone kind, she hoped, someone who loved him.

The man was wearing an identity tag: one of the physios or OTs, Louise thought, until Dad's expression stalled.

'Good to see you!' The man stepped around the side of the bed, right hand extended. Dad responded with his left and they momentarily arced over and under each other, as if performing a secret greeting.

The man's presence made Louise doubly aware of the

lingering smell of faeces and the depressing sight of the other patients, inert like body casts from Pompeii.

'And you must be Phil's daughter – just what we need at times like these, daughters! I'm Adit, from walking football. Andy told me what'd happened and as I work here – radiology, for my sins – I was dispatched to check on the patient . . . So, how *are* you, my friend?'

Dad managed a few moments of bluff camaraderie before his words began to drag: the *tream*, and the *lags*, his *recoverly*. And then he closed his eyes, and she was reminded of a very young and stubborn Max, holing up behind shuttered lids during games of hide and seek.

'I'm sorry,' she said. 'He's exhausted.' And, after Adit had gone, 'You could have told him you were tired and said thanks for coming. That was rude, Dad.'

'I know,' he said.

Back at home, when she passed Max's room on her way to bed, she noticed an electronic glow. She tiptoed along the side of his loft bed and darted a hand between the bars to grab his phone.

'Oi,' he said.

'Oi yourself. You'll be useless in the morning.' She glanced at the screen. It was only YouTube.

He pushed himself up onto his elbows. 'Mum?'

'Yes.'

'Come up for a bit.'

It was late and he had school in the morning. She was about to decline when she felt a beat of regret. Parenthood was a series of codas. She had already said goodbye to baby Max and toddler Max. More farewells were coming; soon the newly teenaged Max would be replaced by adult Max, and he would have better things to do than chat to his mother.

'All right,' she said, and climbed the ladder, the phone stuffed in one armpit, her arms, not used to anything more strenuous than arpeggios and pegging out the washing, pathetically tyrannosaurus-like as they hauled her up.

He made space so she could sit across the bottom of the mattress, back against the wall, feet pointing to the top of the ladder. She remembered sitting at the foot of his old bed which had been smaller and at ground level, listening as he rehearsed his trials and triumphs: handwriting practice versus epic lunchtime games of stuck-in-the-mud.

He leaned over and arranged the duvet so it covered both of them. Then he placed his feet on top of her legs, the vertical to her horizontal.

'What were you watching?'

'A documentary,' he said. 'About this bloke who reckons dead people can be frozen and brought back to life. His Dad died, but he didn't freeze him because you couldn't at the time.'

'Oh. Wow. Can you, now?'

'Yeah, you can. He's really intelligent, the bloke. But I don't think he's thought about it properly. Coming back from the dead could be shit – oi, get off; you say shit all the time. What they do isn't actually freezing. They pump the blood out and replace it with this sort of anti-freeze solution. But if they don't get it totally perfect, you could come back as a vegetable, like, metaphorically and literally, because vegetables change once they're frozen; the cells fill up with water. You could be like a frozen carrot; all soggy. *Un-lucky!* And even if you woke up years later and you *weren't* mushy, there'd be loads of other stuff to worry about. You probably wouldn't have immunity to new diseases. And you'd have no friends. You'd be a defrosted freak. They could keep you as a slave, if they wanted.'

'Well, that's terrifying.'

'Yeah. So is plugging a leaky brain with a ball of metal.'

'True,' she conceded.

'What I really don't get is this: would it – the defrosted brain – be *you*? Would it have your memories and feelings?

Would it be like waking up after a long sleep and thinking, "Oh, here I am, again!" All the stuff that makes you, *you* is, like, in the cells, isn't it? But whereabouts, exactly? Like in the nucleus, or somewhere else? That's what I want to know. And if the living thing isn't really you, is there any point in being alive?'

'I don't know,' she said, wishing she could reward his faith in asking with an answer worth hearing.

She thought about climbing down and telling him to go to sleep, but these chats were increasingly rare, so she waited, the dark sparking her eyes, tiny Catherine-wheels of colour reeling as she blinked.

'I was reading about brain aneurysms and strokes,' he said, finally.

His feet pressed heavy on her legs and she placed her hands on the duvet-covered hill of them.

'There's this idea that when brain cells die they release a tonne of neurotransmitters. And the neurotransmitters can supercharge areas that were previously unused. They, like, *rewire* the parts that are next door to the damaged parts; they're, like, in the *explosion* zone. This one guy, he had really bad damage in the part of his brain that sees motion. But he also started seeing all these extra details. And then he decided to draw them. They're cool. Sort of Spirograph-ish. I can show you, if you like.'

She didn't return his phone. He'd had enough of the electronic glow for one night.

'I'll come with you tomorrow, to see Grandad, shall I?'

'He isn't quite . . .'

'I don't mind.'

'I know.'

'But he minds? Minds *me*?'

'I think . . .'

'I could give him a week to get better at doing stuff.'

'That would be nice,' she said, relieved not to need to push it.

'Nan's not coming over, then?'

'No.' She opened her mouth to comment on the complexities of adult relationships and closed it as she realised he was likely to apply anything she said to herself and David.

'Do you think it'll happen to you one day?'

'What? Oh, you mean Grandad's . . .?'

'If it does, I'll look after you.'

'You shouldn't be worrying about that.' She squeezed the bump of his feet through the covers.

'I'm not,' he said. 'But I thought you might be.' And then he slid down the bed, rolled onto his side and tucked his knees up to his stomach.

She woke when her chin thunked her chest like a piano lid. She shuffled to the edge of the bed, felt for the ladder with her feet and began her descent. When she was halfway down, she turned to face the mattress so she could straighten the duvet. Once Max was properly tucked in, she stepped the rest of the way down and tiptoed across the hall to her own bed.

It wasn't just a matter of learning to do things with his left hand while he strengthened the right. The putting-things-together part of Dad's brain was malfunctioning. The Occupational Therapist suggested jigsaws. Simple ones, to start. And a notebook and pen. In theory, Dad knew what to do with the jigsaw pieces, but in practice he moved them around the bed table. It was like the start of a magic trick, the mixing up part, the shuffling of the deck. Later, he held the pen in his left hand and waited. His grip was fine. It was the words. There were unexpected dead ends during the journey from his brain to his fingertips. 'I know what to do,' he said. 'I *know*.' But the knowledge wouldn't reach his hand.

'Big Kev, Andy and Mike want to come and see you.'

'No,' he said.

'What if it was Kev?' she tried. 'You'd go and see him, wouldn't you? And you wouldn't care if his hand was a bit stiff and his words were slightly squiffy because you're mates. You're on the same team.' The bit about teams, that was genius, she thought. Dad wasn't good on his own, he needed to rub up against other people.

'No,' he said.

'I can't come back tonight, I've got . . . I'm busy, sorry.' It was Watching Week at ballet, but she couldn't tell him that.

'Fine,' he said.

Max's ballet lessons took place in a church hall. Each week Louise parked underneath one of the lancet windows; the escaping light meant she could read in the car. Every ten minutes or so she turned the key in the ignition and luxuriated in the blast of the heating. There wasn't a piano in the hall. The teacher had an iPad, its volume set high enough that, following a burst of heating, Louise sometimes opened the window a crack to better hear the music.

'I don't mind if you stay in the car, like normal,' Max wheedled as she parked up.

'*Un-lucky*,' she said.

The hall was high-ceilinged and draughty. Louise sat on a chair in front of a Victorian radiator, her back hot and her front cold. There wasn't a barre, the pupils used chairs, stacked to the right height. Max had four chairs in his pile, each of the girls – there were six of them – had three. He wouldn't be seen dead in a pair of leggings, so he wore his Liverpool tracksuit bottoms with a plain white T-shirt, and black ballet shoes. While the students performed a lightning quick toe-pointing exercise whose name, *battements glissés*, sounded like a type of cake, Louise used the music recognition App on her phone. 'Mr Brightside' – that's what it said, and she smiled at its mistake, but as the music progressed, she heard the gallop of the transformed melody, a tinkling variation on The Killers' theme.

Max didn't feel the music. Louise watched him during the

piano introductions, arms positioned in preparation; he was stiff, his movements executed with the same lack of nuance and expression she saw in beginner pianists. The girls, though also novices, had been dancing for a term longer, and it showed. Their wrists were graceful, bird-like, as they twisted and weaved at the end of swan-ish arms.

After the barre work she started recording the lesson on her phone. The dancing grew more vigorous and although Max was often half a beat behind the rest of the class, there were things he could do. In particular, a leaping, vaulting dash from one corner of the hall to the other that the students made one after another, after another. This was his forte and he threw himself into it, slicing the square space into a pair of triangles with scissoring legs and expansive arms. When it was his turn to fly back to the near corner of the hall, she felt as if a whole new boy was coming up to meet her.

In the car on the way home he watched her recording. She glanced at his face, illuminated by the glow of the screen. He was smiling.

'I'll email it to you when we get home.'

'I'm so O.P.'

'What's that?'

'Over-powered. O.P at football. O.P on the Xbox. I'm O.P at everything, really.'

'O.P at modesty?'

He grinned and flicked her arm, and she was full of the feeling of *I made him*, full of the pride and wonderment of it.

Usually, the only time Dad sat still was when he was watching sport on the television; an activity that was characterised by an anxious, held-breath calm as he hunkered on the couch like a volcano in waiting. It was hardly relaxing. Even so, Louise suggested that TV might alleviate some of his boredom: someone, somewhere was bound to be playing a game of cricket or rugby or golf worthy of televising. But he didn't fancy it. He had tried looking out of the window when he sat in the chair beside the bed. Following the movement of the passing cars, even for a minute or two, made his eyes and head ache. Watching a screen would be worse, he thought. And the noise, well, he wasn't up to that either. She supposed he was right. There would be the constant drone of commentary, interspersed with applause or cheering. As it was, the intermittent groans of the man in the next-door bed appeared to gallop into Dad's ears before colliding in the middle of his head like a pair of jousting knights.

There was some progress, though. The perimeter of his existence had extended from the double doors at the end of the ward, to the hospital shop, provided Louise or the physio was around to accompany him. And he was allowed, the physio said, to visit the sensory garden on the other side of the staff car park, as long as there was a wheelchair to hand so he could sit if he tired. He wouldn't go, though. He wanted to wait until he could manage the whole walk.

'You don't fancy a shave, Phil?' his favourite nurse asked.

'When I can do it myself,' he said.

'In the meantime, you're going for the hipster look?'

He almost smiled.

In the kitchen Max balanced on the ball of one foot, arms held in first position, and turned. He performed one wobbly rotation, tried again and managed two.

'Not bad,' she said.

'I'd like to see *you* try.'

He opened the drawer and pulled out his turn board, foot-sized and shaped like the rocker on a chair. He fitted his right foot into the curve and pushed off with his left.

'Count!' he called.

'All right. Five, six, seven . . .'

He made nine turns. Arms held high, spinning like an ice skater. When he came to a stop she felt like asking him to do it again because he had looked beautiful and furious and, for a moment, it had seemed that his arms would feather and flap, and he might fly.

She bought a digital watch because Dad couldn't tell the time. But he struggled with the number font and gave it back.

'Don't need it, anyway,' he said.

'Big Kev wants to bring some of the lads. Later, after training.'

'No,' he said.

'There's a card, everyone's signed it. They're worried about you. They'll feel a lot better if they can see you.'

'No.'

'How about if he just brings Dean Edmundson and Billy Carr with him? They're sensible lads. They won't stay long.'

'No.'

'Just Max, then. With me. No one else. David's taking him to training, but I'll collect him afterwards. Bring him back with me.'

He shook his head. His recovery, like Max's dancing, had to be done in secret. It was all very well for him to make the rules, but she was the facilitator, organiser and co-ordinator. She had to carry his phone around with her, fielding texts and calls from mates she knew and mates she didn't, constantly explaining herself – no, explaining *him*. She felt jet-lagged. Time was viscid, her usual routine had expanded to include two hospital visits a day, one after dropping Max at school and another once she'd finished teaching in the evenings. She popped to his house too, usually on the way back from the morning visit, where she picked up the post and the free newspapers and opened the windows for ten minutes.

'Look around,' she hissed. 'You're *so* much better than everyone else on the ward. You can walk and talk. You're still yourself.' In for a penny, she thought. 'You can't hide forever.'

He closed his eyes.

She wanted to say that vulnerability didn't have to be limiting. She wanted to tell him about watching Max at ballet. But she didn't.

She was home from the hospital, watching television in an effort to switch her exhaustion into the kind of tiredness that leads to sleep. The programme was about a woman whose only son had been killed in a car crash.

Max entered the room in his pyjamas. '*Un-lucky*,' he said as he dropped onto the sofa beside her.

'Sorry?'

'You have empathy and that makes you *un-lucky*.'

She looked at him. His cheeks were getting fluffy. One particularly long hair waved from his chin like a seedling.

'What?' he asked. '*What?*'

'You have it too, Max. Empathy.'

'Yeah. Well,' he said.

As the mother in the programme described her son – a *lovely* boy – Louise could feel Max beside her, wanting to say something.

'Grandad's worse than you're letting on, isn't he? That's why you're, like, practically crying in front of the telly. And it's why you won't let me come with you.'

'It really isn't, I promise.'

'Whatever,' he muttered.

She sat in the car outside the church hall, book balanced on the steering wheel. There was an annoying smudge on her glasses. She'd popped into town earlier to buy the new Steven Gerrard book for Dad. And while she was there, she went to the optician's to ask if there was a way of addressing particularly persistent smears. The boy behind the counter examined her glasses and informed her that she had ruined the non-reflective coating, probably by washing the lenses with warm water and soap.

'Oh,' she said. 'But I don't . . . ah, I wear them in the shower. That'll be it.'

'In the shower! Why?'

'So I can see.'

He laughed. 'What's to see in the shower?'

She glanced down at herself and shrugged. But as she walked out of the shop and along the pedestrianised street, she recalled a recent moment when, stepping out of the shower and bending to retrieve her towel from the side of the bath, she had noticed that her breasts were beginning to hang like two tennis balls in a pair of socks. She was ageing; just past the hump of forty and already skidding down the hill – it was now less a feeling than an irrefutable fact. And, with the smooth-skinned boy's laughter echoing in her ears, she wondered who would look after her if she became ill? Who would she allow to see her incapacitated or immobilised? Max? Dad? Neither of them, she thought. No one, in fact. That didn't make her like Dad, though. It was different for her. She wasn't sure how, but it was.

He was out for the count when she arrived. Each time she saw him like that it was a shock to realise that, asleep, he resembled the other people on the ward. She took hold of his right fist and gently unfastened his fingers as he slept.

If he thought he could get away with it, Dad would probably ban her from visiting, too. And hadn't that been her thought when she'd imagined herself in his shoes: to ban him and Max from her bedside?

Louise gently stretched and bent each finger. What if it was her hand? She allowed herself the thought. Considered the deletion of all those practised movements; thousands of hours of rehearsal undone. Piano *training*, Dad had called it. He used to supervise a daily warm-up of scales and arpeggios before she worked on her pieces. And he took her to all her exams because Mum didn't drive. He always waited in the corridor outside the examination room and dissected her performance in the car on the way home. Although he didn't know the correct terminology, he was familiar enough with her repertoire to comment on mistakes made here or there and was sympathetic about the fact that pianists rarely knew the weight of the keys or the press of the pedal in advance: every exam was an away game, played with borrowed kit, he said.

Once he was awake she retrieved the Steven Gerrard biography from her bag and started reading it aloud in a flat scouse drawl which made him smile. But she dropped the accent when she realised that the book's prologue was sad; a description of the low-point of Gerrard's career, his slip during the Chelsea match that probably cost Liverpool the title in 2013/14. After the match Gerrard couldn't stop crying. He was distraught, inconsolable; so distressed he couldn't face going home to his daughters and instead got straight on a plane to somewhere, anywhere. Despite the Liverpool anthem's instruction to walk through a storm, head held high, he felt desperate, and utterly alone.

When Louise reached the end of the prologue and looked up at Dad, he was crying.

Max followed her into the hall, carrying his rucksack.

'I'm coming with you. If you don't let me, I'll just run there after you leave. It'll only take me about half an hour.'

'Oh Max, I don't—'

'Yeah, I know. But I don't care. He's being stupid. I watched the Paralympics with him and he was all, "Aren't people amazing? Never judge someone with a disability." What a hypocrite.'

'Oh, that's harsh.'

With a half-punch from each hand, Max stuffed his fists into the straps of his rucksack. One arm snagged in a doubled-over twist of strap and she watched as he tangled in the fabric, the struggle undermining the effect of his ultimatum. The expression on his face – defiant, flushed – reminded her of something, a memory tucked away somewhere.

They stepped onto the ward. She watched Max's nose wrinkle.

'There he is, on the left, by the window. Go on,' she said.

Dad was asleep. Max approached the bed and stood beside him at its head for a moment before touching his shoulder. Dad woke and pushed himself up using his left hand. And it was done, the seeing; the new impression of Grandad, face maned by the beginnings of a promising beard, expression momentarily panicked as he stuffed the blunt end of his right arm under the sheet.

Max shrugged off his rucksack and sat in the chair beside the bed.

Don't mention frozen brains and defrosted freaks, Louise thought as he retrieved his phone from his pocket. Perhaps he had downloaded something in preparation; a funny clip or the most recent episode of *Match of the Day*. Even better, she realised, would be the recording she had made at ballet.

Dad was saying something. Don't be gruff or rude, she thought. Don't be talking about the reek of the old fellow in the bed next door. Don't say you wish Max hadn't come.

And the memory untucked itself: a football match she'd watched as a child. A penalty was awarded in the dying minutes. It would be the last kick of the game. Dad stepped up. When the ball hit the back of the net, he pulled his shirt off and swung it around his head a few times before holding it out like a bullfighter's jacket. One by one, his teammates ran at him, head first, and he twirled and dodged as Mum, who still came to games back then, muttered, 'Oh, for goodness sake.'

Up dashed Big Kev, luminous in his florescent goalie kit, surprisingly lithe for a bloke his size. He made a couple of feints and then launched himself at Dad. The air thickened with muffled shouts and four-letter words and Dad disappeared under a stack of hairy legs and mud-ringed studs.

'And you,' Mum said, when she told the story, 'you ran at them, shouting, "Get off my Daddy! Get off! Leave him alone! You're *hurting* him." You kicked Kev in the shins when he got up – he thought it was hilarious, of course. Your Dad finally staggered to his feet, all red in the face, he probably *was* hurt – not that he'd ever admit it. And you pointed your finger at them. "You be nice to him," you said. "You be nice." And they listened. If I'd said it, they'd have told me where to go.'

Louise watched as Dad glanced from the phone screen to Max and back again. It was the ballet, wasn't it? That would account for Dad's raised brows. And for the subsequent softening of his expression. He must have seen it, too; the stiffness and missed beats, the scissoring leaps followed by the emergence of a whole new boy. She felt like the middle part of a scale, Dad cradled in one hand, Max in the other. Steady.

Tomorrow, she decided, she'd text Kev and the others and invite them to come. One at a time; no crowds, no pile-ons. She'd stand guard beside the bed and if Dad struggled to his feet, red-faced, she'd be there to support him. 'He's grown a beard during injury time,' she'd say; her words a soft pedal, a means of dampening any reverberations. He'd like that, she thought as she stepped up to the bed.

Eros

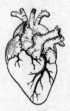

From Ancient Greek

erot- (sexual) love

Love linked to desire; sexual love; romantic love.

Eros is possibly one of the most easily recognised types of love. It's a sexual passion and desire that can come from within or be outwardly directed at a specific person or object. Eros doesn't require emotional fulfilment, but is a physical craving.

The Love Story

Grace McCleen

She lives with her mother and father. They live in a terrace. At the end of a terrace, in a grey house in a grey town. In a cold, damp country. Her father is a builder. Her mother is a housewife. They live a strict and frugal life. Though her father takes them out, sometimes, for tea, or to stay in grand hotels that are miles away from the house and the town. Though he owns a string of classic cars that change regularly and that are as out of place in their street as a pair of velvet slippers in a skip.

She does not have company. None of them do. Her mother does not have friends she meets up with and nor does her father. They do not really fit into the small greyish town. They are not greyish – and nor are they small. Each of them, are actually quite big. And they each live in a rich, expansive, counter-world; her father of bygone days of grammar schools, rock and roll, classic convertibles; scarved, flare-skirted, pony-tailed girls. Her mother in a world of school boaters, lacrosse, musicals, cookery, painting and embroidery. In fact how her mother and father ended up in this town is a mystery. Part of the explanation is that they chose menial jobs, for various reasons. But that is only part of the mystery. Another part is why they chose each other.

Her father does not seem to mind that they are here and are not the same as their neighbours. He works like a Trojan, earns good money and buys another car, a different suit, a new pair of brogues. Her mother does not mind it either. She bakes, cooks, cleans and keeps house. She decorates the house, paints the cast-iron bath, stencils borders, makes curtains and coats and dresses; hangs dried flowers from the beams her father has exposed, plays the old black upright piano that stands by the French doors her father put in the front room; she does countless things other mothers she knows never do: preserves fruit, plays with her and makes things for her toys; reads her stories. Her father has never played with her or made something for her or read a book with her; he has never even entered her bedroom, at least not that she can remember.

Her parents do not mind that they are different from others. She does. She finds children laughing at her or whispering about her in school and comes home crying. Her mother gets very worried. Her father is not even aware of it. But she can't really do anything about it. She supposes she could try not to be top of her class, but it would not really make a difference; she would still be different.

She does not go out and play with other children. She plays in her room, though it is not really playing at all. In fact the activity she is engaged in within these walls is exacting and involved: she arranges her toy animals and dolls in one scene after another, scenes that take weeks to stage. She creates stories for them that take even longer. She has never reached the end of a story because they take so long to tell and because she puts so much detail into them. She comes in from school, goes upstairs, and begins talking in an undertone. Or, if the scene is not yet ready for the latest story, she continues to create it. Mostly she tells love stories between men and women.

One day she reads a book that makes her feel something inside her has opened, something that has long been shut; she almost feels she has remembered something she has forgotten, though why that should be she doesn't know. She does not like the book much. It feels bland, to her; unsavoury, alien and imitative in comparison to her other well-loved tales. Yet the central conceit strikes her as brilliant: the hero, a boy, spends the entire story searching for a girl, who happens to be a princess, only to discover at the conclusion that he *is* the girl; that he – or she – was turned into a boy by a witch when he/she was a baby. In order to be transformed back into the girl who is really himself the boy must die. This is the tragedy, because this boy is all that the child knows of himself; the boy is his entire self. Yet it never really existed. If you fall in love, she wonders, and it is reciprocated, is it like finding that other self without having to give up your own? Or is it like losing yourself, but in a good way, a way that does not feel like a loss? She is sure, already, at eight, that if she fell in love the other problems in her life would recede into the background. Love is the answer. Of this she is sure.

She has noticed that recently, when she tells her love stories, even when she is staging them and has not yet reached the point of telling them, she feels what seems closest to say is an itching, flickering energy throughout her body. Her heart thuds – so hard it makes her feel dizzy. This never used to happen and she does not tell anyone about it; for some reason knows she mustn't. What worries her most is that it is not a loving feeling her love stories evoke – not the sort of emotion she feels towards her mother, for example; not a desire to cherish and protect, a quiet pleasure, a generous warmth; but a violent, urgent emotion – perhaps not really an emotion at all, but a sensation – like hunger or thirst. She assumes that when she experiences romantic love herself she will also feel the caring that is supposed to go along with it; that surely her parents feel, or felt, for one another. Though when she tries to imagine this she cannot. She can more readily imagine her father feeling this wild feeling she has recently been feeling than tenderness. It is difficult to know how he feels about her mother; he shouts at her, he tells her to move faster, to hold this, take that; he screams at her sometimes, when she drops something. She has seen her mother crying in her bedroom and did not let on she knew. As she watched her mother cry her stomach descended, and continued to descend; lower and lower – through the centre of the earth it seemed – then on again, into the blackness of space. This, she imagines, is the opposite of how love must feel.

At other times her father brings home flowers, makes her mother laugh so hard that she cries, holds out his little finger – at the dining table, as they are walking, as they drive along in the MG or the Jaguar, the Sunbeam Talbot or the Triumph Herald, the hood down, The Gypsy Kings playing, sailing through the wild and beautiful and haunting evening air; glorious, disquieting, endless countryside; her father will extend his little finger for her mother to hold; and she will; while he talks nonsense to her, calls her 'Creature', himself 'Monster', herself 'Ems'; he will say: 'All right there in the back, Ems?' And she will beam and nod.

Whatever love is or is not, and whatever story she is telling about it in her bedroom, running through it all there is a soundtrack, supplied by her father's music cassettes, which he lets her borrow to play on her own tape recorder. She listens to The Drifters, Bobby Darin, Perry Como, The Beach Boys, Buddy Holly, The Shadows, Chris Farlowe, Gary Puckett, Little Richard. In time, Love has a sound. It is 'Going Loco Down in Acapulco', 'Under the Boardwalk', 'Rain and Tears', 'Save the Last Dance for Me', 'Dizzy', 'Take You Where the Music's Playing'. It also has a landscape: a blue crêpe-paper sea, boardwalks and promenades made from lollipop sticks, whittled surf boards, sand she persuaded her father to give her, palms made from the tops of feather dusters and pine-apples, very green faux grass, short white garden lights with little cardboard roofs lining paths, a round swimming pool she has made from her mother's embroidery press. In her room there are malls and Cadillacs and sidewalks, hot-dog stands, ice cream and Orangina stands (the last, an enormous orange she hollowed and fitted with a small bar). Above it all a white sun dangles – a light bulb veiled behind gauze; the love light.

*

The landscape in her room is not like anything she has actually seen, but it fits the music, and seems a plausible place where love might happen. There are other landscapes of love, she imagines, too; darker ones, tied up with pain and an almost unbearable sense of loss; moonlit gardens of country houses, great lawns, fragrant shrubs, ancient trees, ornate terraces. But she does not make this landscape; she makes that which accompanies the feverish, exciting love, that takes place by the sea, beneath blue skies, in brilliant sunshine; a world lit more brightly than daylight. When she finally begins a story, after preparing for it for weeks, her heart speeds up. She can smell the sweetness of plastic shops and plastic cafés, plastic horses and cars, plastic parks; the heady perfume of the dolls' furniture, hair, bodies. She sometimes wonders if she will ever encounter this landscape in reality; whether it even exists, or is just in her head.

In her stories, lovers are separated by fate and united. Dolls wander vast deserts (the empty middle bedroom her mother has not yet decorated), sleep in the shelter of rocks, the woman doll riding by day with her baby on the back of a horse, slipping forwards with exhaustion, the man stumbling on with the aid of a staff. A beautiful doll with long raven hair reaching to her knees, amethyst eyes and skin the colour of caramel, is an island girl forbidden to meet the sailor doll by her tribes people. Two other dolls, in the present day, walking a Scottie and Red Setter dog, meet in a tangle of leads, only to lose one another's phone numbers. Another pair meet at a party, but the male doll is already married so they cannot do anything. There are a real lack of male dolls. She has to make do with a placid, dreamy, blue-green-eyed and slightly squinting male that the toy companies obviously think little girls want to play with. The doll's chest is like a bar of chocolate, his biceps perennially tensed, his hands shaped in a manly grip, palms cupped, thumbs curving slightly backwards. He *is* more or less her ideal, except that he is too pretty, too effeminate. If only his expression was a little darker. If only he were less pretty, looked less like a boy.

There are other disadvantages to plastic. No matter how blue the crêpe-paper sea, realistic the beach or pink the Cadillac, the scenes feel contrived. No matter how brilliant the light in her bedroom, it does not really feel like sunlight. Her love stories are serious; they deal with affairs, with bereavements, long illness, surgical operations, childbirth, Braxton Hicks contractions, life-threatening injuries, care of disabled children. But no matter how wet she makes the dolls' hair they never look as though they are sweating; no matter how she positions their bodies and heads they never look devastated. She has to put their stupidly straight or stupidly curved hands across their mouths or turn their heads away or let their hair cover part of their face to denote any emotion other than blank contentment. The inflexibility of their limbs (and the female dolls' concrete breasts) thwart intimate arrangements. Their knees do not even bend enough to make them look as though they are realistically sitting – a fact she has become so exasperated by that she forced their legs to bend further, resulting in at least one doll whose pale, grey, plastic ligaments have popped through her rubbery skin and now cannot be ignored. What would real love feel like? Skin to skin, heat to heat?

The stories she tells about love have never reached an end – most not even a wedding – and so are never consummated. Physical consummation of love, she believes, can only occur after marriage. And the consummation of love is all she is really interested in. One evening she spends hours describing a kiss. She had staged the scene over several days: the male, half-blue, half-green-eyed doll, and the girl doll with the dark-red hair stand beneath the fake Gypsophila her mother bought for her and is meant to look like a blossom tree. She made the utmost possible use of their unbending arms, their resistant bodies, the limited movement of their heads. She bends the redheaded doll backwards slightly at the waist; makes the man doll cup her head in his hands. The redheaded doll's other hand is flung out a little because she was overwhelmed by the passion of the kiss and because her hand would not bend around the man convincingly. The challenge was to suggest a moment of intense yet controlled passion – and she *felt* that passion as she arranged the scene, her stomach turning, light-headed, her heart beating so powerfully she feels sure she is moving slightly to and fro. Yet when she comes to narrate the kiss, the amount of words she had to use, the numerous attempts to do so because she was disturbed (by dinner, by a group of youths loitering by the railings below her window, by the bin men arriving later that night); the long preparation for what was, narratively, no more than a few seconds, meant that even as she described the moment it became worn and unreal. If only she could experience love herself, know it first hand; know the moment all her stories lead up to, including this, and not have to narrate anything at all! If only she could experience not just the kiss but what the kiss is leading to (and what this might be she is not sure, exactly, has only a vague idea); not travel towards love any longer, but to arrive.

She is careful to dismantle the trysts after she has staged them in case her mother sees. She is not sure why this would be devastating, only that it would – and something they could never talk about – they who talk about everything else. It must be something to do with the feverishness she feels when she stages them. Is the thrilling, overpowering sense of anticipation that is simultaneously satisfied and simultaneously deferred – is that love? Or is the excitement simply because she knows it is wrong? But why is it wrong? When did it become so?

One winter, the winter she is nine, they go there, the place in the songs, the place she has been making the whole time, or as close as damn it; a place with glittering sea, miles of beaches, boardwalks, palms, promenades, esplanades, cocktail bars, ice-cream stands, palms, Orangina stalls; and more – marble foyers, fountains, stone lions, glass-walled corridors, gift shops, dining rooms, ballrooms, lounges with tapestries and pianos and suits of armour; green lawns that appear to vibrate beneath water-sprinklers, a multitude of swimming pools, terraces, walkways, bridges – there are even lights along the garden paths with little roofs like she made for her dolls! And above it all a white, pulsing sun; hidden not behind gauze, but a real haze of heat and light.

But there is more: many of the singers in all of those songs on her father's music cassettes have stayed in this very place! She sees their photographs adorning the mirrored walls when they descend the spiral staircase to the dining room every evening: Frank and Dean-o, Sammy and Gerry, Bobby and Buddy, Ricky and Little Richard; that band, this group; this duo, that quartet. These singers have touched the same surfaces she is touching! It is almost laughable how like her template of love the place is.

For the first few days her parents hold hands everywhere. They go down for drinks at 'Happy Hour'. Her father asks and her mother plays the baby grand in one of the lounges. Sometimes she holds her parents' hands and they swing her, big though she is. For the first few days, whether because he too has finally arrived in this place, beneath a sun he talks about each freezing winter at home and now beats down relentlessly on his pale arms, chest and legs where he sits in the white plastic chair on the balcony or lies spread-eagled on the sun lounger by the pool he has nabbed before the Germans can, her father is more at peace than she has ever known him. At dinner, his hair combed into an aggressive D.A., the marks of the teeth still visible; ruddy, handsome; smelling of Brut and toothpaste, rough and spruce in his cravat and tweed, he lets her mother hold his little finger across the table. He lets her hold his other little finger too; 'Finger!' he says, in a silly voice, and she holds his stubby, red, mottled finger, which though his smallest finger, requires all of her own to enclose.

After breakfast they spend the day in the hotel gardens or stroll along the *carihuela* to the town before heading back to the room to bathe and dress for dinner. After dinner, in the black, washing night, they walk along the seafront again, in moonlight balmy as an afternoon, beside a sea restless and tossing, past closed amusement arcades, merry-go-rounds and crazy-golf. Young couples, still as statues, sit at comically regular intervals along the sea wall. The couples are oblivious to their passage, lost in one another's eyes or gazing out upon the world unseeing, but her body becomes unbearably tense as each couple grows closer, to the point where she thinks she will trip, and sometimes does. A heat she is afraid her mother will notice pervades her body, her chest becomes tight. As they pass, her body subsides into normalcy again. Why this tension? Is it because what the couples are doing is wrong (surely nearly all of them are unmarried; her parents are clear that any romantic activity should be contained within the bounds of the marriage arrangement? Is it because she is witnessing their displays of affection in the presence of her parents? Is it because *she* wants to be partaking in such activity? If she was alone would she feel this discomfort?

'We've gone past that stage now, haven't we?' her father says to her mother, hand in hand with her mother.

'I don't know if we ever went through it,' her mother says wryly.

But she hopes she goes through it – wrong or not, un-chaperoned or not; she hopes this suddenly more than anything she has wished for yet in her life, though she does not know why. And she hopes that this 'stage', as her father called it, will last; she hopes always to be in that intense, feverish state of fierce anticipation, simultaneous craving and satiation; if she does not go through this state, if she does not taste this ravishment, this strange, alien, half-alarming enchantment; this – *love?* – if she does not at some point *know* this, then she would rather not live; life will have been for nothing.

And she knows that she will, of course, like every other woman. And men already like her: the owner of the restaurant which serves fresh fish says he will steal her away in his car, the owner of the hotel bar asks her if she will marry him, the handsome receptionist smiles at her dazzlingly when she learns enough Spanish to ask for the room key – so dazzlingly it is as if she has been stabbed. The waiters in the dining room call her 'guapa', 'bella', 'bonita'. They wink at her, chuck her cheek, rest shocking, cool hands on her neck. The feelings these attentions provoke are part alarm, part euphoria; part sickness, part sadness; longing and having all rolled into one.

One evening they see two young couples enter the foyer and cross to the reception desk. The couples are tanned and good-looking and she wonders if they are married or not. The men have their arms around the women's shoulders and when they have obtained their keys and entered the elevator and the elevator doors seal themselves behind them they leave a bow-wave of fun, thrill and airy freedom that expands and goes on expanding in the lobby. When she is older *she* will come to a place like this on her honeymoon; she will be in love here. She will drive up with her love in an open-topped car and they will walk across to the reception with the same ease and style – because this is love, too; this effortless happiness, this stylish grace. And in time it will be hers. But after the elevator disappears she feels a surprising jolt of fear – or is it grief? And why that should be she doesn't know.

Her father spends the first week with them. Then he can bear it no longer, assembles his bike and leaves for the mountains before breakfast, returning just in time for dinner, drunk with sunlight, exhaustion and endorphins. He has sprigs of almond blossom for her mother, a small, bitter orange for herself, and that evening in the dining room, over plate after heaped plate, he regales them with tales of leaving the rest of the cyclists behind, battlements and village squares whose beauty brought tears to his eyes, beer colder than any he has tasted before, of bocadillos with paper-thin ham cut straight from a bone in front of him and hot chocolate thick as syrup in a small bar with a dusty, marbled floor that no tourist has ever discovered before.

While her father is away her mother reads, sunbathes, helps her with homework, sketches and paints. They go to the town or wander in and out of the souvenir shops on the carihuela, debate about buying some toy or other, eat secret bags of crisps from the small *Supermacado*, not telling her father at dinner, who permits only dry bread and 'naranja' between. The naranja taste wild and violent. The streets of the town begin to seem dead, or dying, like the boats hauled up on the shore, their underbellies exposed and peeling. Things begin to seem empty or wrong. Without her father something is missing.

Her mother helps her compose stories for the dolls. A good story can take many days to alight on. Then she and her mother look for the perfect place, which can also take days, where her arrangement will not be discovered or disturbed. When they find it, her mother leaves her and sits a safe distance away, and she begins to tell the love story, only for someone to pass by or look at her and ruin it. Then begins again the process of making a new story, finding a new place.

As long as the sun shines her father cycles. As long as he cycles he is happy. As long as he is happy her mother is too, or appears to be. And she should be too; she should at least be able to tell the perfect love story, here, where everything she imagined for so long, and made – out of whatever even roughly approximated it – has turned out to be real. Often, however, she cannot even begin a story. The sun is too hot to move around in; too hot, it feels, to breathe. It is too bright, even when she is wearing sunglasses. She had not banked on real sunshine being such hard work. The paths and beach are too hot to walk on. She did not think that real things would be this difficult to work with. Sometimes she does not want to arrange the dolls or tell stories at all. This too is surprising. She is feeling more and more dissatisfied with them. Sometimes she lies back in the middle of what at home would have been a key scene, closes her eyes and sees how long she can bear the sun on them, the simultaneous pleasure and sickness and itch; till weeping, she rolls over, wiping the water away from them, her nose burning. Sometimes they go up to the room because of the sun. It does not seem to be the same sun here as at home. It is dark even while it is bright, or so bright that it feels dark. Or is the darkness just a feeling? With this sun there is little build-up; it is simply overhead – and it stays overhead all day. Then, just as swiftly, it descends at night. There is no story with this sun. It will not allow it.

The sun upsets her stomach. It makes her dizzy. It makes her uneasy. To evade it she wanders hallways, dabbles her fingers in fountains, tiptoes through tiled courtyards and into rooms where long curtains are drawn against the midday glare; touches the fingertips of suits of armour, gazes at murals of bullfights and armies, rearing horses, the frilled skirts of dancers. Everything in life, or most things, seem to be pitted against something else; there is always an opposite. Why is that? Is that where the excitement lies; excitement the same as the love feeling? Does the matador feel the same flurry of feelings she feels when staging a love story when he thrusts the rapier into the bull's back? She does not remember ever noticing how so many different things feel before; ever noticing her skin or her body so much. She slips through shady lounges heavy with the smell of leather and tobacco, peers into rooms draped in white sheets, follows the sinews of marbled floors, steps back into the blazing sunlight, breaks open cactus leaves, tastes the clear glue on her tongue; trails her knuckles along textured plaster and rubs her back against coconut palms, catches the stray kittens who live in the bushes beneath the dining-room balcony and feels their infinite softness and beneath the softness beating hearts; tiptoes over scalding sand, the cold, slippery raised concrete near the pool; through freezing, shooting water.

One afternoon, two weeks into the holiday, she begins to ache. Her abdomen throbs, pulses. She cannot think of a better word to describe the sensation than 'ticking'. Some tiny mechanism low down in her body seems to be flicking or jumping, counting down to detonation, a countdown she is finding it hard to ignore. Three days later, in an attempt to find the source of the ticking, she locks herself in the shade of the bathroom and inserts a small silver pencil between her legs. The ticking increases, as does the aching, though it is not really aching now but more of a pulling, hand over hand, towards something or other. And some thing or other intensifies then dissipates as she moves the pencil further in. Not knowing what else to do, she extracts, washes it, and trembling so much she can hardly unlock the bathroom door, reappears in the bedroom. Her mother is still reading on the balcony. She does not appear to know what she has done. But does she? Why should it matter? Is what she has done wrong? She cannot say explicitly that it is. Why then this reaction? What does she know? What has she done?

There comes a week when everything is grey and storms batter the palms and *carihuela*. At breakfast the waiters are glum-faced, almost surly. They stand looking out at the weather, towels slung over their shoulders, arms full of plates and shake their heads. They do not even have a kind word or a wink for her. After breakfast they go to one of the lounges, where her father sits turning the pages of a newspaper noisily. Later he walks stony-faced with them beneath dripping vines that overhang back streets, over pavement tiles sliced into innumerable small squares, past shops barred by grilles. Her eyes pass over square after square, grille after grille. Perhaps that is what she should do with her story; divide it into lines or into boxes; decide what information should be conveyed each day; make up a timetable and plan. Otherwise it will be time to go home and she will still not have told it.

One wet afternoon the hotel put on a screening of *The Quiet Man* in one of the lounges and she and her parents watch the titular John Wayne wrestle then kiss the soaking Maureen O'Hara – the most beautiful woman she has ever seen, ever since the first moment she appears in a headscarf with her sheep. She understands the thrall Maureen has over John Wayne's soul. She understands why he can think of nothing but her. In fact, O'Hara bears a striking resemblance to her favourite redheaded doll, Marie. Unlike Marie, Maureen is hyper-real; larger than life between pillars in the darkness of the lounge, in the stone hut deep in the wet, Irish countryside. She feels hyper-real Maureen's ribs rise and fall as she is seized by Wayne, feels the graze of his wet jaw as he forces his kiss upon her, and notices the same throbbing, the same sickness, the same aching once more inside her, as relentless as the wind and rain that batter the hut door. She thought it was the sun but it can't be because there is no sun here, and has not been for days.

The storm recedes, the sun returns, her father rides mountains on his bike. Her mother embroiders, reads, swims with her in the pool or the sea. She arranges the dolls and begins again with a new story inspired by the storm, but yet again she fails to finish even the first scene. And to get to the key scene, the real reason for all of this, she must reach the point where the dolls are married, yet so often, for some reason, she resents this fact; does not want the dolls to be married, and not just because it takes so long to reach this point in the narrative (in fact she has never arrived there) but because the act of consummation will not be as exciting when the dolls are married. Why is this, when, after marriage, people supposedly love each other for sure and have pledged they will do so forever? At what more perfect point could the love act occur? In any case she still does not know what the love act actually involves, only which parts of the body and the most rudimentary motions; and of course, the dolls lack precisely these parts. Marie has nipples – discreet ones, barely traceable – but nipples all the same. The man doll, he has a large vertical bulge in his crotch (presumably to look authentic when dressed in the swimming trunks that he came with) but which itself seems like a garment, some sort of covering. That is all. She presses the dolls together when it comes to the act itself. Apart from that she does not know what else to do. Yet when she does, the ticking low in her body accelerates to such a degree she looks around to see if her mother is there, before turning back to the dolls and moving them against one another; what else is there to do? And now there is heat low down in her body too, like the sun when it beats on her head or her eyes and she sees how long she can stand the pleasure and sickness and itching. When it is over she rearranges the dolls into innocent poses again, glancing all around her, then waits for the sensation to subside.

She feels she is getting closer to something, approaching the lip of a waterfall, hearing someone say: 'Warmer . . . warmer . . .'; walking forwards not knowing what she is going to discover.

The ticking forces itself upon her attention more and more. Waiting for her parents to get ready for dinner, the slop of soapy water coming from the bathroom, her father's dangerous, wild-smelling aftershave, palms scratching the balcony rail, the distant sounds of splashing and cries of late swimmers from the pool below and further away from the beach, 'Sealed with a Kiss' coming from the two mini speakers she sometimes uses for her dolls' discos plugged into his Walkman, it is here again: this sensation which seems to be one with this place that she knew before they ever arrived – one with the feeling of the dark sun on her head, the echo of the foyer, the clamour of the dining room, the din of the kitchens when the double doors swing open, the swash of the sea, the particular polish the cleaning women in their backless clogs use to clean the corridors, the way the fan is moving now above her head; what *is* it? Is it close by or far away? Sickness? Sadness? Wanting? Having? Losing? Finding?

She closes her eyes. The singer's voice – how can she describe it? 'Wily'. 'Crooning'. 'Yearning'. Yes – the voice is yearning. 'Burning' – and yes, it feels like that to her as well. Another song begins. 'With all the charms of a woman – oo-oo-oo-ooh', sings Gary Puckett, 'You kept the secrets of your youth – mm-mm-mm-mm . . . You led me to believe, you're old enough, to give me love, and now it hurts to know the truth – woh-woh-who . . .' She picks up the cassette cover. Her father, lobster-red from his bath, elbows on his knees, is peeling a 'naranja' with his cruel-looking fingers and long, flat, rounded nails. He looks up sharply as she touches the cassette but says nothing for the moment. The girl on the cover is freckled, heavy-lashed, snub-nosed. She wears long socks and a short dress that looks like something a baby might wear. She has a fringe and ponytail and a ribbon in her hair. How old is she? Surely not much older than herself. Would Gary Puckett sing this song to *her*? Perhaps the sensations she has been feeling over the past days is how a woman feels. They are not altogether pleasant, but they are certainly exciting. She flushes and places the cassette back on the dressing table, but her father has not noticed any change in her; he is turning his head to rip chunks of orange flesh from the rind, long blunt incisors flashing beneath his moustache. She glances at her mother, who, having applied her makeup, is now straining to tong the back of her hair in the mirror. Her mother's mouth is contorted. She looks at once grown-up and childlike; no – she looks like a teenager. Her father's tearing at the orange now seems to be related to her mother in some way. Sadness washes through her like sand. She goes onto the balcony and leans her forehead against it, letting the breeze caress her arms and shoulders.

There are ten days till they leave. The heat continues but the sun does not reappear. The sky is thunderous. She is heavy and listless. She gives up telling stories with the dolls or thinking of new ones. She rubs two ceramic ornaments together, a bride and groom that her mother bought for her at one of the gift shops in the town. The ornaments' faces are perpetually surprised, their small lips pursed in 'o's. Their bodies will not meld but chink awkwardly, the bride stubbornly clasps her flowers in front of her; the groom unhelpfully folds his hands across his chest. She feels a rush of disgust, or is it desire? Something flares and burns darkly inside her. Her hands are shaking. Is this the feeling two people have when they 'make love', as the songs say? When they have 'sexual intercourse', as the dictionary says? Or 'fuck', as the kids say in school?

There are eight days until they leave. She feels congested, compacted, close to tears for no apparent reason. She and her parents go searching for a pottery along dusty motorways then walk along a road smelling of herbs and wild flowers, cutting across the land as darkness approaches, to rest on broken pieces of sewage-pipe and brick as they wait for a bus to take them home. Another day they walk out to some marshes, passing windmills whose sails thrash the air to see flamingos rise in a pink and black cloud. That evening, in a room full of people, her parents do something she has never seen them do before: dance to live music and she bursts into tears, trying to separate them like a small child, clawing at her father, then runs out into the dark gardens.

There are five days till they leave. There are four. There are three. She and her mother take themselves out for the day in spite of her father, who stares thunderously at them when they announce their plan, catching the horse and cart driven by a man with a chest as hairy as a doormat that stops outside the hotel. The cart drops them further away from their destination than they had expected and they spend two hours walking. Midday, overwhelmed by heat, they sit on a kerb. As soon as they have reached the town they have to return to the place where they must catch the horse and cart. Back at the hotel they do not tell her father their mistake but instead describe how fun the outing was.

There are two days till they leave. There is one. She looks at the dolls where they lie, smiling stupidly skywards. Sometimes she wishes she could break them but her mother would see it and she cannot let that happen. Why did she ever think she would be able to tell the perfect love story here? It was much better at home when everything was pretend. Life will not turn out like that, will it? It will not turn out to be better when experienced as a story that never materialises but always promises satisfaction? She is tired of having to tell this part and never that part; she is tired of never arriving.

She is treading water in the indoor pool on the last evening while the sun sinks like a neon blood orange into the sea. Her mother is reading on the lounger. Her father is somewhere.

She prefers the pool at this time of day because it is often empty. She hangs, treading water in front of the place where warm water gushes from a vent in the side. Palms outside tap their papery fingers against the windows. The kitchen fans have begun to whir. She can hear the distant clash of pans as the evening meal is prepared. At this time tomorrow they will be on an aeroplane. Their strange sojourn will be over.

It will be good to go home now. She is homesick, she realises. All this strangeness, this excitement, this longing – for
what? This sadness? This continual promise without fulfilment? She will be glad to leave it behind now; be swallowed
once more by the concrete and humdrum. This place was not
the perfect place for her story; it was the worst; she has never
been less able to tell love stories than here. The whole place
suddenly seems like a betrayal – though of whom, and what
she supposed that it promised, she is not sure.

She closes her eyes and the water pummels her body until
she no longer knows what is her body and what is the water,
and after a little while she becomes aware that she is crying,
tears making their silly way down her face, even though her
eyes are closed. Then there is another sensation: sickly,
hallowed, blinding, blackened; no images, no sounds, no narrative, no storyteller. It rises from the centre of her body and
she is impaled upon the sensation and, suddenly terrified, tries
to escape it, snatching at the tiles in front of her, even as she
attempts to rise, going under; coming up again; it mounts
higher; sun-sickness, madness; an unbearable, heinous, hideous
pleasure that threatens to annihilate her; that puts her nowhere
and everywhere, strung throughout time – and suspended in
no time at all; only now: wave upon wave upon wave; and
she crests and buckles and breaks into shards of unimaginable,
unendurable joy.

When she wakes she is wiped out, the world darker. She
scrambles out, grazing her shin on the steps and not noticing,
running and skidding towards the woman reading at the other
end of the pool, pulling on wet clothes, talking constantly
through chattering teeth, sitting while her mother helps her,
wondering if she knows, the world scattered and burning,
knowing things that were hidden, that this is what songs, what
stories, talk about, this is the end of the stirrings, the touches,
the warnings; this is the knowledge, weeping that it was known,

Agape

From Hellenistic Greek

agap- love

*The highest form of love; love equated with
charity; unconditional love; altruistic.*

Agape love is unconditional and unspecific. It
neither wavers, nor falters; it is a transcendental
love that is constant and charitable. Replete with
forgiveness and patience, it's often associated with
religious connotations of love as it's linked to love
for humanity as a whole.

The Human World

Bernardine Evaristo

If there's one thing I can't stand it's the way people see fit
to perpetuate an image of me that is not accurate. As nobody
has ever seen me in the flesh, it's all conjecture anyway. Much
to my chagrin, the most enduring image portrays me as an
old white man with kindly blue eyes, a flowing white beard,
wearing a flowing white robe. Typical patriarchal bullshit,
right? When I look at myself in the mirror this is *not* what
I see. What I see is a gorgeously voluptuous negress sporting
a dazzling afro and wearing a psychedelic caftan à la 1960s.

And why not? I dress to please myself, obviously. I know
that some of you will denounce this image as the work of a
storyteller's sacrilegious imagination. Others will say that the
very concept of a divine being is a fiction, a fantasy, a fanciful
idea. They will deny that I exist at all. They will say that
humans needed to come up with creation myths about how
the world came into being because they didn't understand the
notion of evolution via the growth of organisms. They will
say that over time different versions of me emerged as a figment
of the collective imagination. Well, I'm proud to say that this
particular 'fictional character' has lasted longer than many of
the other incarnations. Anyone worship Zeus these days? Or
Amun? How about Oshun or Cerridwen?

In some parts of the world my sphere of influence predom-
inated for centuries because long before social media went
viral, my spiritual philosophy got there first. Not that it lasted.
Nothing ever does. I know this because I've seen that everything
on the planet is in motion, transient, ever changing. Human
populations move with the times, as do their spiritual needs.

Still, it's with a deep sadness that I acknowledge that out of some seven billion souls inhabiting Planet Earth in the twenty-first century, the majority don't acknowledge even the idea of me. Worse, some of those who do appear to follow me are among those who exemplify the worst kind of false-piety, who use my name to justify the most bigoted attitudes and heinous crimes, who think that going to church every week elevates them onto the moral high ground, when inside their hearts are . . . rancid.

Religious hypocrites abound, pure and simple, and they do nothing for my reputation. Does it upset me? Yes. Can I do anything about it? I try. Am I myself perfect? Judge for yourself.

I often nostalgically reminisce about the Golden Age of the Crusades when my emissaries went forth into the world to convert pagans. It's true that blood was shed in my name but that was beyond my control. Believe me, it really was. I might have established the Faith but I cannot control how people use and abuse it. It's also true that missionaries were sent out to pacify the pre-colonials to lay the ground for the military who went in with guns to colonise them. Also *not* my responsibility. If only people knew that while I was as omnipresent and omniscient as I could be, at least before technology fucked everything up, I wasn't *omnipotent*. In Lucifer I have long had a formidable foe.

My mission has always been a good one – to instil a moral code into the populace, to help them differentiate between right and wrong and thereby make them better, nicer people – people who want to share more of the love and less of the hate. Now some of you might think I'm being way too judge-mental, and too right, I am. I have to be because I have supreme moral authority and also, I am supposed to be *honest*, right? Without a moral template, people tend to give in to their baser instincts. That said, I have managed to head off countless conflicts for which I receive little credit or appreciation, I have to say. Having a word in the ear of warlords helps, both the kind who are legitimate political leaders in democracies *and* the outlaws red-eyed from chewing khat who ride down out of the mountains brandishing both sabres and AK47s. And my attempts to stop those intent on expanding their murderous and genocidal endeavours has staved off greater casualties than the world has hitherto witnessed. Imagine 200 million people dying in the Second World War, instead of the 60 million on record, and you get my drift.

I am very proud of the fact that I have, at times, managed to rein in some of the worst excesses of human nature. Humans are fundamentally flawed (Adam/Eve/Snake/Apple), and without my influence as a leading light of the worldwide spiritual movement, you really would have decimated your race by now. *One race*, that was only ever the intention – the *human* one.

And it is the human race that is my responsibility, which makes my job the most demanding and impossible ever conceived. If you doubt this, you imagine trying to enlighten humanity 24/7 from Evolution to Eternity. It got so bad that I decided some years ago to reduce my workload to eighteen hours a day. I needed a break. I needed to sleep. I felt myself going crazy thinking irrational and paranoid thoughts and started to feel deeply resentful of helping people who never thanked me. I subsequently researched alternative options that would assist me with my task, and negotiated a deal via the internet for a discounted job lot of superfast screens that would allow me to tune in to the world in its entirety – via satellite wireless connection. It was, I admit, an admission of failure from my original intent, which was to see and understand all things simultaneously since the Beginning of Time, but if I had to reduce working hours and scale back on the scope of my ambitions in order to stay in the game, so be it.

Unfortunately, this is what staying in the game entails: Unreasonable Job Description (tick); Huge Moral Responsibility (tick); Formidable Opponent (tick); Reduced Popular Appeal (tick); Paedophile Priests' Nightmare *Ongoing* (tick); Personal Image Misrepresentation (tick); Disappointment in Humanity (tick); No support network (tick); Loneliness (tick).

While I *am* lonely, I do appreciate my home. I really do. I live in a lovely airborne capsule that orbits the globe in outer space – powered by solar energy. I wake up on my waterbed each morning (GMT) feeling myself floating, usually with the light of the disappearing moon shining in on me. If I've had a restful night sleeping, which isn't always the case when I'm disturbed by nightmares about the terrible things happening down below, I feel good, energised, ready to get going with saving the world. If my sleep was disturbed, as it was last night because I'd spent the day focusing on child abuse which really, *really* gets to me, I wake up feeling like shit.

First I go into my walk-in shower and wash myself in the goodness of refreshing, reinvigorating water, grateful that I've never gone without it. I'm so aware that still today there are people on earth who do not have enough of it, who walk miles a day to fetch pails of it for washing and drinking, people who have died in droughts that last months or even years. Famine is one of my biggest worries, especially with global warming on the rise, in spite of the naysayers who deny that it is. I dread to think what will happen when it again hits one of the world's hottest and poorest countries.

Once I've moisturised my hair and teased it out, and dressed myself in my chosen colourful kaftan of the day, I walk barefoot into my self-cleaning space-age kitchen with its sparkling steel surfaces. I make myself a kale, blueberry and yoghurt smoothie in my juicer, purchased online at a very reasonable rate. It's the latest breakfast fad that I've picked up from watching videos of health gurus in California in my down time; people who clearly don't believe in food very much at all. I wonder how long it will be before I crave my usual delicious fry-up of eggs, sausages, bacon, mushrooms, tomatoes, baked beans and pancake with maple syrup. It might be bad for the arteries, but that's not a problem because I have been blessed, or cursed, depending on my mood, with eternal life. I have no idea what it feels like to be human, to know that one day there will be an end to my life and to know that I cannot control how or when it will happen.

The smoothie gives me a boost of energy and helps me think more clearly. The fry-up, on the other hand, satisfies me emotionally. I know, comfort eating. You'll shortly see why.

Next I walk through my spacious inner sanctum of beautifully curved white Perspex walls towards my study. It's very feng-shui, very harmonious. Once there, I sit at my desk constructed from 2,000-year-old Galilean wood by a carpenter called Joseph as a special present to me upon the birth of his son. (I managed to find it on eBay quite recently.) His son claimed to be me on earth, which was fine because he kickstarted Christianity which mass-marketed my ideas. I'll not quibble with it. He was a preacher-man, for sure.

On the wall facing my desk is a galaxy of computer screens stacked up in vertical and horizontal rows of ten. One hundred screens in total. It really is the most effective and time-efficient way to keep an eye on the revolving planet below. I turn the screens on from my remote control.

Next I park myself on my ergonomic Herman Miller office chair, which helps me sit straight. It's another indulgence but I reckon that I, of all personages, deserve to sit in comfort to carry out my never-ending stream of duties. My job is necessarily a sedentary one. I am the ultimate professional couch potato and I'd noticed I was becoming hunched some time ago and sought to correct it.

I begin to watch the screens, each one flowing with a never-ending stream of images. I mute the sound and stop on images that demand my attention. I feel like some kind of ultra-security guard surveying over seven billion people getting up to whatever they're getting up to. It is morning and afternoon, it is evening and it is night – all across the world. As the sun sinks in one part, it is rising in another. It is dark and it is light and all the shades in between. It is Arabian Peninsula hot and Antarctica ice cap cold and every temperature permutation on the planet. The full spectrum of the human race is on my screens: all cultures, all ages. Some people are just being born, others are coming to the end of their lives or are already dead.

I do what I can, case by case, screen by screen, watching out for those moments when I can make an intervention, a word in someone's ear that might save someone or whole groups of people from a terrible wrongdoing, calamity or tragedy; a word in someone's ear that might give them hope, to get them through their tribulations – to hang on, to forgive, to think positively about every situation no matter how dire, to see the light at the end of the tunnel.

After yesterday's focus on the rescue of children from paedophiles, those who have and act on urges most humans cannot comprehend, it's hard not to return to the scenes of the crime, to check up on the little ones. Children are so close to my heart because in them lies the survival of the human race. Children are the future. Naturally, I found it happening or about to happen everywhere. Inside all kinds of homes, in nurseries, schools, medical facilities, temples of worship, places of entertainment, at the shops. I found it in the great outdoors: woods, parks, beaches, mountains. I find it happening in cars, vans, trucks, trains, buses. I needed to capture the attention of the perpetrators before the deed was done. How do you stop someone from pursuing their own twisted sexual gratification at the expense of a vulnerable young child who is, in that moment, unprotected?

I had a word with them, which is all I ever do. I try to stir their consciences, make them realise that it's in their power to make good choices that do not hurt anyone else. I cannot force people to do what they don't want to do. I can't make miracles happen. And here's the thing: nobody can. (Now you know.) Oh but you shop online, I can hear you protest. Now while that's true, it's merely a way for the universe to provide for me.

The truth is, I am not a magician. Like I said, I did not wave my magic wand to create the world; it created itself.

I tell those paedophiles to listen to their better selves and desist, and then I have to listen to their usual bollocks in response. How their urges are beyond their control. How the child is asking for it, likes it, is old enough to be inducted into sex by a caring individual. How it's not sex but love. I try to get inside the perpetrators' heads and make them imagine their own faces superimposed onto their victim's. This works when there is enough self-love not to self-harm.

Or to imagine the face of a child they would never hurt, not even under the pretence of loving it. Better still, if I can make them imagine the child's pain before the deed has been committed, or to imagine the psychological legacy of the abuse in later years. These strategies work in sixty per cent of cases.

These paedophiles are usually seen as perfectly 'respectable' sons, fathers and grandfathers by their communities. Often they are family men of the old-fashioned kind. I approve of families, stable ones, which are necessary for what they now call 'social cohesion', but I detest the notion of family values only equating to a man, woman and their children. I detest the notion of one kind of family taking the moral high ground over the others. One parent and one child is a family in my opinion; two women or two men co-parenting is a family; or a daddy who is now a mummy or a mummy who is now a daddy. I might have lived a long time but I am not old-fashioned. I keep up with the issues of the day and what matters most to me is that children are raised by loving parents who properly protect and nurture them. There are good families out there, and there are bad families out there, and there are bad men who are following Lucifer to hell. Damn them.

I must get on with today's work instead of wallowing in what happened yesterday but anything less than an 80 per cent success rate always bugs me. I watch the screens and feel my brain cells powering up, multiplying and connecting with the people of the planet below. I am alive with it. I feel as if flashes of lightning are shooting inside of me and I become super-charged with millions of currents emanating from me as I plug myself into those people in the world who need my help.

I connect myself to those who are living in dictatorships where they are forced to regard their leaders as invincible demi-gods, to societies where its citizens have to abide by the edicts of their leaders whose word is law, societies where books, music, films and media are banned other than those approved by the government that perpetuate the party line, which keeps the people ignorant, which keeps the people brain-washed, which ensures they know only what the government wants them to know, which insulates them from the social and political progress made in other parts of the world, soci-eties where people are not allowed to think for themselves and suffer terribly as a result, their minds repressed to the point of mental inertia and capitulation, to the point of believing they have no agency, and if they do question their leaders, or even criticise them privately among friends who turn out to be spies or in rooms that are bugged, they and their families are killed, tortured or banished to a life of hard labour in prison camps where they die from malnutrition, overwork and brutal punishments.

I connect myself to people in societies where the tyrants pass their political leadership onto their children, as if it is their automatic inheritance, leaders who treat their countries as their own private property, who treat the country's treasury as their own private income which is lodged in tax havens, who build palaces for themselves instead of hospitals for the sick and dying, who do not build schools for the majority of the population who are illiterate, who do not invest in businesses or agriculture or new and improved infrastructures that will improve their citizens' quality of life, but who will, instead, allow their wives to plunder state funds in order to fly private jets to buy more shoes, clothes and jewels than they can possibly ever wear from the designer heavens of Europe and New York.

I connect to people in societies where the caste hierarchy of culture, colour, religion and class put at a disadvantage those who are considered inferior, societies where those who are at the top of the tree are given every opportunity, advantage and privilege, and told that they are more important, more worthy, more deserving, more special, even more human than those considered underneath them – the lower castes who are told that they are there to be menial, to be marginal, to be no-paid or low-paid, who are punished and derided for being poor, people who are denied access to all the good things society has to offer because of their caste, not because they are not good enough, not hardworking enough, not clever enough, not talented enough, societies where people try to survive by any means necessary.

I connect to people in societies where those who are low caste are persecuted by the police, the military, the secret services, where those who are low caste are unfairly prosecuted and adjudged guilty for being the consequences of their own unequal societies, whether they are guilty or not, who are incarcerated in prisons where they are the majority, where they are more harshly sentenced than those who are considered higher caste for committing the same crimes, those who end up in prisons that are run by the state and who end up in prisons that are run by private companies whose high profits correlate to the high incarceration rate, people who are sentenced by judges who have shares in the prisons, judges who mete out harsher, more unjust, sentences to the weak who do not have the funds to fight back with the best and most effective lawyers, judges who mete out harsh sentences knowing it's more money in the piggy bank – for them.

I connect to societies where children are forced to go to work in factories making cheap clothes for the West, where they are forced to spend their childhood mining gold or diamonds, or working at brick kilns or employed as child soldiers in rebel armies and bandit brigades where they are given narcotics to numb them from their own pain and the pain of others.

I connect to societies where education is banned for girls, where women are not allowed to be outside the home without a man, where women are subject to the jurisdiction of their husbands, or their fathers or brothers or male Elders, where women are not allowed to work in most professions, where a husband beating a wife for insurrection is considered good practice, where women are genitally mutilated because sexual pleasure for a woman is disallowed, where women are not allowed to speak up, let alone to answer back, where women are not allowed to wear what they like, where they are forced to cover up their entire bodies when they do not want to, who are told that they are seductive temptresses whose bodies must be hidden from the sight of men, even when they are girl children.

I connect to societies where women are burned to death because their in-laws demanded more money for the wedding even after the agreed dowry had been paid in full, societies where girls are forced to marry men who are four, five, six, seven times their age, who die of internal injuries on their wedding nights, who have babies so young their organs cannot take the strain, or their pelvis breaks, whose bodies break down so that both mother and child die in childbirth, societies where girls grow into women who are sexually abused because their bodies are considered to be for the pleasure of men, by men who do not understand that their sexual pleasure comes second to a woman's right to choose with whom she has sex, and how, societies where women are trafficked across the globe and forced into prostitution, forced to have sex with strangers who come into their rooms all day, every day, for years without end, who detach their minds from their physical selves, who become addicted to drugs, who are threatened with the death of family back home if they try and leave.

I connect to women who are trafficked to work as domestic servants but are never paid, whose passports are withheld by their employers, who are stripped of their rights, who cannot leave the homes of their masters, who work long hours and are on call the rest of the time, who are called domestic servants but are, in reality, slaves.

I connect to societies where the conquering militia force people to convert to other faiths – or die, societies where people live in fear of leaving their front door in case they are randomly arrested for not being of the same religion, or for not being of the same sect of the same religion as the rebels who have taken over their town, people who fear being labelled subversive, or who are punished for having a relative who spoke out against the regime.

I connect to societies where people fear imprisonment for not applauding when a corpse is dragged through the city centre behind a truck, where people are punished for looking at soldiers in the face when they pass them in the street, which is seen as antagonistic, or for looking the other way when they pass them in the street, which is considered disrespectful.

I connect to those societies where hundreds of schoolgirls are abducted and never again found, who become lost to their families, who have been forced to abandon their education, forced to marry rebel soldiers, forced to convert to the religion of their captors, forced to become their brides, forced to have their children.

I connect to those societies where all young men have to be conscripted into the army and may not see their families for months or even years, conscription that can last their entire lives, that has no get-out, no end of non-contract in sight, where men who desert the army are put in front of a firing squad of unwilling conscripts such as themselves, unwilling conscripts who are ordered to discharge bullets to stop the hearts of their fellow soldiers.

I connect to societies where women who are lesbians suffer correctional gang rape by men who think lesbians are the ones who are mentally and morally sick.

I connect to societies where gay people are lynched by the mob who burn down their homes, drag them out onto the street and tear their bodies apart with machetes.

I connect myself to those societies where men are thrown off the roofs of buildings for being homosexual, to those societies where gay men are flogged and imprisoned at best, officially executed at worst, according to the country's constitution for the crime and sin of not being heterosexual.

I connect to people in societies where hands and feet are amputated as punishments for theft, where people are beheaded for a criminal offence, where women are flogged for having an affair, or flogged for sex outside marriage, or flogged for accusing a man of rape, or – who are buried up to their heads and then stoned to death with bricks and rocks.

I connect to those fleeing societies who have been arrested and are hoisted backwards into the air by their hands and ankles for days, where their body parts are burned with fire or acid, their nails are slowly ripped out, where they are beaten with batons and cables, or water-boarded, their ears cut off, their tongues cut out, their anal and vaginal passages assaulted with objects, man-made and human, rifles and knives and rods, where their eyes are gouged out, their balls electrocuted, their insides disembowelled.

The day rolls on and I roll with it, plugging into the thousands of humans who flee societies where it is better to risk death by trying to escape rather than stay where the quality of life has been degraded beyond the point of survival, where people are dying of starvation, where people lack a decent provision of medical attention, where they risk death by the government, death by the rebel armies, death by other government, death by other governments who bomb the hell out of them – military and civilian alike, where they risk having their heads impaled on a stake outside the city gates, where the men who rule instil a fear so great that whole populations are in trauma, where every single expectation to a human right has been eroded, where they try to raise the money to escape the badlands, selling everything they have, leaving a house that was once a home that has already been torched to the ground, where people who leave become refugees calling on the compassion of the human race to help them out of hell.

I watch them flee the badlands, not only for a better, more liveable way of life but just to stay alive in itself, I watch them flee the dictatorships, the religious fanatics, the mass rapes of young women, the mass graves of older women hidden deep in the woods, I watch them flee by day, flee by night, fleeing for their lives, fleeing the border guards who have to be bribed but might change their mind on a whim, I watch some of them make it to the towns outside the Sahara where they are supposed to be guided across it by smugglers who might get them to the other side, or who might not actually know the routes across the desert, or who give up and abandon their charges who will die of dehydration after three days without water, or once they do make it across the ocean of sand, who might renege on their financial agreement and demand a bigger fee than previously negotiated, who will torture them until their families send additional retrospective payments.

I connect to people from these societies who are packed too tightly onto trucks too small for the purpose, I see them try to get past the bandits, the militias, the border guards, who might or might not allow them passage, I see them packed into boats built for a quarter of its escaping passengers because the smugglers are pursuing the biggest profit margin possible, I see people packed into holds where they shit where they sit, where they throw up over each other and cannot clean themselves and cannot escape the stench and the heat and the sickness that spreads – for days and days while dreading that their boat will never make it to the land mass on the other side, the continent where they hope they will be safe.

I see people who are ill tossed over the side, I see irate individuals who will not sit quietly, tossed over the side, I see ships capsize and the unlucky ones sink, I see ships calling for help and help arriving too late or not at all, I see thousands dying, I see women, I see children, I see men, hundreds upon hundreds, thousands upon thousands, going to their watery grave, I see some of them washed up onto the shores of Europe.

I see most countries shutting down their borders, not taking their share of those who are fleeing, absolving themselves of all compassion and responsibility, I see the former colonial mega-empires not acknowledging their culpability in its global project of colonialism, how it exploited whole continents for their resources, how wealth was siphoned off to its colonial heartlands to form the economic bedrock of its economic stability and prosperity, how it created false borders, false nations, gave rise to false leaders, how it tore communities apart and forced hostile societies to co-exist when they should have been kept apart.

I see the culpability of international banking and trans-national business and their role in propping up dictators, their role in trading with autocratic regimes, their role in debt collection, I see governments whose overriding ambition is to negotiate the most favourable price for the commodities that provide the energy upon which their countries rely, I see countries going to war to protect the pipeline to the west, I see them making a dog's dinner out of Reconstruction. I see societies imploding into civil war.

I have a word with those who blame the persecuted for trying to escape their oppressors, the very oppressors to whom their governments have supplied the machinery of their autoc-racy – armaments, I have a word with the money-men, the middle-men, the border men, the smugglers who exploit the situation but are not its cause, the governments who do not want refugees to sully their shores, the media and politicians and pundits who scapegoat those who are fleeing and blame them for everything that is going wrong in their own country, even though little goes wrong in their own country, relatively speaking, because their countries are in the world's top ten per cent for wealth and standard of living, or even in the world's 'Top 10', I have a word with those public figures who decry the refugees as vermin, swarms, cockroaches and scum.

I have a word with societies that can accommodate more of those who are fleeing societies in the world's bottom ten per cent for quality of life and standard of living, who don't realise how lucky they are, who don't realise that opening their gates to more refugees won't precipitate a cataclysmic economic decline.

I look out on a planet that has a tribalism at its core, a tribalism that has prevailed ever since it came into being. People, animals, insects, all life is, by nature, protectionist: protecting the family, protecting the home territory from outsiders, protecting economic interests that allow one's own citizens to survive, to flourish.

I see it is easier for millions of people to grieve for a single pop star who has just died, than it is to pay any attention to the millions suffering terrible hardships in the world today. One celebrity death is emotionally containable. The pain on the planet is not.

It is my job to go on with this work, this is my duty, this is my calling, even when my implorations fall on deaf ears, even when I despair that not enough members of the human race want to save everyone else on the planet who needs it, as I had once hoped – that goodness would out, even when I see that it is in human nature to only want to save themselves and those whom they love.

I am a force for the greater good. I am the imagined

embodiment of the higher selves of humans. I am capable of love and compassion for all humanity. It is my role in life to try and save *everyone* – often from themselves and most certainly from each other.

As my working day ends, I feel quite exhausted and drained, every day is different, every day is packed with images and events where I step in and try to help. I am not complaining, not really. I might bang on about my unreasonable job description but there is such personal satisfaction when things work out, when I witness the many acts of kindness, of unselfishness, of compassion, of charity, that saves and improves lives, that make me believe there is hope for the human race.

This is not a jeremiad. Our world has improved. There is progress in every aspect of society that would have been unimaginable a hundred years ago, let alone a thousand. More people are doing better in their lives than are not. But there is also regression. It is the law of nature, right? Two steps forward, one step backwards on the road to civilization. I understand it, but I do not understand the Deep Web which hides itself encoded beneath the surface of the internet and makes it hard to track the source of websites that operate illegally. It has changed the game.

The Deep Web makes my job all the more difficult in tracking child abusers and it makes their objectives so much easier to realise. To this I return. To these humans who go cyber-subterranean to unleash the monster inside of them. Damn these paedophiles who use the web to traffic children to each other in the virtual and the real world. It's so hard to work out which computer connects to which website when there are hundreds of thousands and even millions of them at it – posting and viewing and taking advice from each other on the most effective ways to groom an adult to get at a child.

Here I am, floating around the world in outer space but with no idea how to decipher cyberspace to get at the culprits.

It keeps me awake at night. Like last night. How can I access humans who have made themselves invisible?

Years ago technology consisted of using wood and flint to make weapons, and rubbing sticks together over dry grass to make fire. Today? It pains me to admit it but for now, the Deep Web has outwitted me.

I seek out some calming music being played somewhere on earth on my screens. A live recital or concert will help me unwind. There are always plenty to choose from, usually played really badly by amateurs. Luckily, I come across a professional recital of Satie's *Gymnopédie No 1* at the Royal Albert Hall. I tune in and turn up the volume. It is exquisite. I shut down all the other screens – one by one the people of the world disappear. They'll have to get along without me until tomorrow morning. I just hope that nobody presses the nuclear button between now and then.

The music slows down my mind and soothes my heart. I light up a menthol cigarette, and pour a gin and tonic from my drinks cabinet. My little vices. I think I deserve it, don't you?

I walk over to the curved windows of my spacious capsule that look out onto the atmosphere. The darkness out there is so beautiful. So peaceful.

I look out onto the stars, over a hundred billion of them in the galaxy they call the Milky Way, 32 billion light years from earth. There are billions more galaxies in the universe, thousands of them have been catalogued. Andromeda, Cosmos Redshift 7, Centaurus A, Large Megallanic Cloud, Whirlpool. Yet we still know so little about them, about what is out there.

I look out and wonder. I wonder if there exist other beings with powers greater than my own. I wonder if I too am being watched.

SceptreLoves

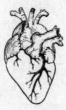

The hardback publication of *How Much the Heart Can Hold* was heralded by the SceptreLoves short story prize. The following story by Phoebe Roy is the winning entry.

#SceptreLoves

It Was Summer

Phoebe Roy

It was summer, and Michael couldn't sleep, because Michael had met a boy. It was past three in the morning, and he sat on the seat under the big bay window in his living room with his knees drawn up to his chest, clenching and unclenching his fist to reveal the crumpled-up napkin with Dev's number written on it. The napkin was getting woolly and the ink was blurring from the sweat on his palm, and every time he opened his hand it swelled softly as if it were breathing.

Dev had written his name and number down in large sweeping script and handed the napkin over, then he'd touched the centre of Michael's chin with one thumb and walked away.

Michael was the kind of man who appreciated this kind of flourish, and hated the idea of pecking his number, calculator-like, into someone's phone. Michael hated the modern way of most things – he wrote cheques, and used paper maps, and played tapes in the car. Even though Dev himself had seemed very much a modern invention, he was the first thing that Michael had seen when he entered the gallery where they'd met, and he'd occupied his gaze in a way the art had failed to.

Dev stood out in the crowded room like a sunlit cathedral in a silent square. He was slim and sharp, with hair so glossy it looked like that of the plastic doll Michael's sister had had as a toddler; he wore expensive glasses and a charcoal suit. He probably did all his banking through his phone, and knew how to make his life easier, and ease made Michael uneasy. Unfurling the napkin, and dialling Dev's number to ask if he could take him to dinner would be the easiest thing in the world.

Michael uncrumpled it and smoothed it out across his thigh

153

to study Dev's writing. The seven was larger than the other digits in the phone number with a decisive line crossed through it, and he'd put a kiss under his name. In the morning, Michael decided, crumpling the napkin back up, he would call him.

The first time they had dinner together, Michael had a nervous energy that made him feel lighter and clumsier than usual. He kept dropping his fork on the floor and fumbling over his drink, and flinching whenever Dev lightly touched his wrist. He found himself disagreeing with Dev for no reason, over things that didn't matter to him, because Dev had turned out to be the sort of man who bristled quickly and forgave even quicker and Michael wanted to see him snarl. He wondered if he made the same face when he came, or if his eyes would glitter like that if he were watching Michael undress.

Dev leaned back in his chair to watch him as he paid the bill, and suggested that they leave with a graceful gesture. Outside on the street, under a sharp navy night, Michael found he was too shy to look directly at Dev and instead held his breath and smiled anxiously over his head, which was easy since Michael was at least six inches taller. He smiled at a dog out for its evening walk, and Dev twisted his wrist and placed his palm gently on the side of Michael's throat, his fingertips sliding into his hair.

'I want to take you home,' said Dev. It was summer and Michael said yes.

It was summer and Michael and Dev were driving to the beach on a peach-and-mint morning, the light blurry and the shadows sharp. Michael had persuaded Dev to take a day off work, and had confiscated his phone to stop him from sneaking emails. The phone was on the back seat, wedged between Michael's overnight bag and a picnic cooler and Dev kept turning round to check it was safe.

'The phone's not our child,' said Michael, after Dev had craned round for the fifth time. 'Look at this weather! Look at the hills!'

Dev obediently turned to look out at the flat country unfolding like a road in a video game in front of them. The sky was like roses seen through milk and Michael's joints felt warm and loose, both from happiness and exhaustion. Dev plucked Michael's hand off the steering wheel and kissed it, and Michael glanced down and then over, but his passenger had already gone back to looking outside the car. The street lamps flew past the window and then disappeared behind them, as if they were falling off the edge of the earth. Then they reappeared, and the world kept turning.

Michael still wasn't sleeping well, but this was less indecision and more because Dev now stayed over most nights and he operated a curious internal thermostat which made his skin begin to burn a few moments after he fell asleep. The night before, Michael had crept out of bed with a throw round his shoulders and Dev had immediately uncurled in his sleep like a deep-sea creature shaking off the day in luminous folds, and stretched out in the centre. Michael had squatted down next to him and kissed his boiling forehead. Dev didn't wake, but smiled and parted his lips, and Michael had been suddenly fearful. The thought of the day that Dev would smile for the last time and then die had gripped Michael's stomach like an eagle's talons closing over prey, and he got back into bed and arranged himself around Dev's star-fished limbs.

Dev had stirred and mumbled.

'What's the matter?' he asked, lifting his head.

Michael sighed, and said he didn't know. This wasn't quite true, because he did and he didn't. He always found that summer was too much for him. The concrete smelled too much of stone. Late at night, a memory hung from every ink-dark cloud.

'Tomorrow, let's go to the sea,' he'd whispered in Dev's ear. Dev agreed, and told him to go back to sleep, so that was what he did.

*

It was barely seven in the morning when Michael and Dev arrived at the seaside, and the car park was dew-shimmery, like the skin of some large mythical animal. As he got out of the car and breathed in salt and rock, Michael's stomach lurched as if there truly was a loping animal beneath him, and his fingers stole up to check the truth of his jaw, to press his lips, to rake through his hair. He reached for Dev and closed his hand over his wrist, which had chilled in the daylight.

'Are you alright, sweetheart?' asked Dev. To Michael he seemed bigger than he was, his face specially commissioned and customised. His smell mingled with the ocean crash in Michael's nostrils and his pulse was steady as an anchor. He was the only thing Michael saw. Michael nodded, and the grin he gave Dev was stripped back and honest, showing all his teeth because he wanted Dev to see them. He wanted Dev to see all of him.

He took a photograph of Dev standing like a watchful statue, ankle-deep in the surf, and fussed around him with a towel when he emerged grinning from the water, gleaming shell fragments clinging to his feet and ankles like acolytes. They lay together on the sand as the sun climbed and shone so brightly it was almost black. The gulls screamed and Dev rolled over on his side and threw one leg over both of Michael's.

It was summer and Michael didn't want to spend time with anyone who wasn't Dev and Dev felt the same, so they began to live like romantic wild children. At the weekends they stayed in bed until three in the afternoon, and had picnics on either of their bedroom floors.

One afternoon they went on a complicated bus journey to a suburban shopping centre to buy Dev a bike lock (he wanted to pick one up locally, but Michael insisted it would be an adventure), and they picked alongside the main road like adventurers in the July heat. Their eyes were sore and delicate from too much time spent in darkened rooms, and the grass by the side of the road was dried and brown, but they were both serene and lightheaded from not drinking enough water.

When they got back to Dev's house, a huge ramshackle Victorian with cupboards that didn't close properly, Michael clutching in his fist the bag that held the bike lock, they undressed and lay under the window. Eventually, Dev spoke.

'What I'd like is for the gallery to mount an exhibition about rooftops,' he said. 'The secret world of rooftops.' Michael's eyes followed where Dev pointed, to the red roofs and the chimney tops and the roosting pigeons and the people sunbathing.

'There's only one secret world I care about,' said Michael, and made a cup shape with his palm and dragged it down Dev's chest, over his curved ribcage and where his hip bone sloped gently down, until it hovered around the triangle described by his thigh tops. Heat filled Michael's palm, and Dev breathed sharply in before telling Michael that he was unbearably pretentious but oh god how he loved him. Oh god, how he loved him.

It was summer and they went to the riverside and drank cold wine, and visited an overgrown graveyard, and read the newspaper with Michael's feet in Dev's lap, and watched the shadows moving across the walls, and they pretended that these moments added together could make up the whole of a life. When they had administrative tasks to do, they turned them into games, and the way they spoke was so laden with reference, allusion and private jokes that none of their friends could stand to be around them. This was fine by them – Michael thought that he could live forever sustained by only the salt he licked from Dev's skin.

They went to a daytime screening of *The Apartment* one blue August day, and had the cinema all to themselves. They stayed tilting their faces up to the screen long after black replaced Jack Lemmon and Shirley MacLaine dealing out their gin cards, Michael's hand clasped loosely over Dev's knee. They breathed in the smell of aged upholstery and toast and coffee and warm vinegar softened up by dust and Dev suddenly gripped hold of Michael's arm and spoke into the darkness.

'Don't leave me,' he said.

'Never,' said Michael.

It was autumn and Michael and Dev started getting up on Saturdays when the alarm went off instead of staying in bed, and they went for long walks in the orange-and-gold parks, and started spending time with their friends again. They went on short breaks, and longer ones to Paris and Prague, each surprised that the other had such strong views about the correct time to arrive at an airport before a flight. The abrasions of daily contact had shrunk them both, and Dev no longer filled Michael's vision and perceptions. He was no longer almost afraid to touch him. This made Michael sorrowful, but he was also relieved that he could get back to work and stop leaving the laundry.

Even though the restoration of routine relieved him, Michael missed their liminal twilight existence and the way Dev's bedroom smelled in the daytime of sleep and lavender milk and warm cotton. He burnt an incense stick in the box room he used as a study to bring Dev to mind when he was at work at the gallery. They watched Scandinavian detective shows together and made complicated soups and stews in Michael's tiny black-and-white-tiled kitchen.

Michael's grandmother died, and they went to Dorset for the funeral, Dev looking more glamorous in his new Marc Jacobs suit than strictly necessary. They fought about this in low hisses behind a gravestone. Michael caught the flu, and Dev took the week off work to look after him. It occurred to him that he could die, but every time he tried to get a grip on this thought his vision blurred and tilted, and he felt as if the back of his head had turned to syrup. He hunched his shoulders against the sensation of unprotected skin, and spat into one of Dev's jewel-coloured water glasses that he'd brought round the month before, saying Michael's were too depressing to drink from. On the day his fever broke, Michael woke to find his flat clean and sparkling, with a bunch of tulips on the windowsill and a note with a list of things to pick up for supper.

It was autumn, and Michael had had his new manuscript rejected by his editor. Dev bought him a bottle of his favourite whisky, and arranged him on the sofa under a blanket like an invalid, but Michael did not want to be consoled.

'Write another one,' said Dev.

'You would say that,' said Michael. 'Anyway, this is your fault. You said it was a "good start", which is a terrible thing to say anyway, but then you never gave me any proper notes.'

Michael knew very well that he'd always insisted that Dev's job was to offer unconditional praise, and Dev knew this too, but he didn't argue. Instead he gave Michael one long, level look, and left the room. Michael returned to looking for clues as to either his deep genius or his fundamental failures of character in the email his editor had sent. By evening Dev and Michael were friends again, but Michael couldn't help but feel that he'd revealed something he hadn't meant to, something desperate and grimacing, a baring of teeth.

It was autumn, and for the first time Dev went to sleep without kissing Michael good night. Michael lay awake until dawn warmed the curtains, his eyes dry and itchy, his heart in his throat, the light from the street lamp making a golden pool under the cornicing, his palm gripped uselessly around Dev's wordless upper arm.

It was winter, and Dev and Michael were packing to go to one of Dev's two sisters' wedding. Michael's mouth was set in a grim line, because Dev had joked that next season they'd have to go to someone's baby-naming ceremony, and Michael thought that this was a cheap thing to say. He was infuriated by the bookend symmetry of the wedding and his grandmother's funeral in the autumn and he couldn't bear it when Dev said cheap things, or when he left his bag in the middle of the floor. Dev couldn't bear it when Michael followed him around switching off lights and putting coasters down or the way he liked to try and guess the next line of dialogue in the cinema.

'Shoes at the bottom, socks in the shoes, jumpers rolled up,' said Michael, leaning over to fix Dev's case, which gave a teetering impression of a cloth archaeology. Dev batted Michael's hands away and continued to fling items into the case in a carefree way. Michael watched for a while longer and said, 'I love everything about you, except for the way you pack.' And Dev said, 'I love the way you tip your whole head down when you look at me.' Michael reached out for the sweater that he knew from experience Dev was about to fold poorly, which Dev gladly handed over.

'Thank you *jaan*,' he said. A fierce demanding joy drew Michael's ribs in, that Dev would call him *jaan*, and he tried to think of a way to answer. In the end, he said, 'We'll have to get the winter bedding down soon,' and hoped it conveyed the same, even though he knew that Dev felt obscurely that sheets were more romantic. Dev didn't say so, though – just chuckled, called Michael 'grandma' and went to find the car keys.

They kept up their game of each saying what they loved about the other in the car, throwing love smoothly back and forth between them like a tennis ball, both pretending that it wouldn't matter if either of them dropped it. Making their avowals out loud was a deliberate tending of neglected grass, a careful husbandry, even when they ran out of meaningful things to say and began instead to praise each other's wrists and handwriting.

By the time they arrived in Solihull and were greeted by Dev's parents and his other sister, their eyes were dreamy and their cheeks were sore from smiling. Dev's mother removed her hands from where they were jammed into the opposite sleeve of her cardigan and gave Michael a hug. She told Dev to remember that his aunties all thought he'd left the gallery and was training to be a doctor, and Michael glanced over at Dev nervously, compassionately, ready to console, before he saw him grin and roll his eyes and realised that she'd been joking.

At the wedding, Dev's aunties pinched Michael's cheeks and pressed food on him, and one told him that she was happy that someone at last would bring some height to the family. 'Your kids will be nice and tall, ha?' she said, and then she and the other aunties began to cackle, although not unkindly, and their jewels shone in the dim marquee light.

Although Dev had promised him he wouldn't be forced to dance, an auntie seized Michael and dragged him into the centre of the floor, where she laughed at his attempts to keep up. His long limbs and back only looked graceful when either still or lounging and he was surprised when he didn't mind. He liked Dev's family, and their friends, and their friends' families, and smiled weakly at the children who asked if he was Uncle Dev's husband. He plucked at his suit and watched Dev dancing, feeling briefly abandoned, but then Dev clapped his hands together and laughed at something his sister said, and the feeling faded and resolved itself as tenderness.

Under a guest duvet cover in Dev's childhood bedroom, Michael gripped Dev by the waist and pressed a kiss to each of his hips. Dev wound his fingers in Michael's hair, and said, 'I want to fuck you.' Between kisses, Michael said, 'Yes. But do it quietly.' They both laughed, and their laughter was caught in the moonlight coming through where the curtains didn't quite meet. It striped the floor and their bodies, and it muffled their sighs and whispers.

The next morning Dev's mother woke them with a gentle knock at the door and tea. When they emerged squinting, Dev's father was hovering on the landing, where he shook Michael's hand and invited him to come and look under the bonnet of his new car. In the evening, Dev's parents suggested they watch their favourite American police procedural with them, and Michael sat obediently on the sofa between Dev's mother and father, while Dev and his sister wrestled with their ancient DVD player. It was winter and the blue light from the TV bounced off Dev's back and made his edges shine, making him seem as if he were crouching in a fall of pure new snow. It was winter and they decided to spend Christmas apart, New Year together, and, finally, time after that apart.

In the months that followed, neither could say who had pulled the final thread that unravelled them, but Michael was certain that it had been Dev who had said, 'If you want to leave, then leave.' They both knew other things too. Dev knew that Michael had sent a box of his possessions to the gallery only two days afterward, packed so neatly it seemed a deliberate affront, and Michael knew that Dev still hadn't read his book. Things they didn't know: that Michael had kept back Dev's old Aston Villa shirt and kept it folded under his pillow, and that Dev could barely hear Michael's name without a lump forming in his throat and a little flurry of heartbroken heat spreading across his back. It was winter and neither of them knew that the other still slept as if they weren't alone.

It was spring, and Michael began a writer's residency at a nearby school. He went to the opening of Dev's 'rooftops of London' exhibition, and drank oily white wine in a corner with one of Dev's sisters, who claimed to be allergic to this much culture. Dev was wearing one of his suits, and cut through Michael's vision like a knife of light. As always, he seemed to show an unusual organisation and collectedness of body. Even as he zipped around the room he was somehow stiller and more distinct than everyone else. Dev glanced at Michael, scowling in the corner, and his heart and stomach gave a tug when he saw the flakes of dry skin between Michael's brows. It showed he'd stopped taking proper care of himself since the painful conversation they'd had just after the New Year.

Michael went into school, and worked on the redraft of the manuscript his editor had rejected, and wrote a play about the Tolpuddle Martyrs. He met friends for drinks and went to see his family, where he helped his father paint the front of their house. It was spring and he stretched his hands out in front of him and peered at the curious geometry of his skin cells and the blue-green of his veins and wondered if he was expected to go on just living side by side with himself until the day he died. His memories became impolite and nudging, popping into his head fully formed and without warning, and he had to pretend he was suffering from early hayfever when tears came to sting him. Dev, laughing at a video of a man trying to dive into a frozen pond; Michael trying to teach Dev how to correctly peel a carrot, and Dev cutting his finger and the running tapwater swelling the blooming blood into a pale red jewel before it burst and fell into the sink; Dev, his teeth gritted and his head thrown back, sunlight gilding his edges like the pages of an expensive book.

Dev tried to work out where his assistant had filed the customs declarations forms, and went on a date with a friend of his sister, who showed him seventeen identical pictures of a mountain he'd climbed. From time to time he thought of calling Michael, just to chat, just to see, but he remembered how he'd looked at the opening and put it off, then put it off again until it would have looked strange. In the end he didn't need to concern himself, because towards the middle of April Michael called and invited Dev to his birthday drinks. Dev went, and was surprised at how warmly he was greeted by Michael's friends; when he spoke to Michael, the conviviality was a little forced, their laughter a little loud.

'So what have you been up to?' said Michael. Dev admitted he'd been seeing something of the friend of his sister, with the pictures of the mountain, and Michael's smile twitched and faltered before he remembered himself and strove to wear it all the more broadly.

'Great! Would love to meet him,' he lied, and gulped his drink.

'You'd hate him,' said Dev, and looked down at his own glass, then back up at Michael's throat moving. 'You look good,' he said.

The next morning Michael examined the purple bruises that

blossomed on his thighs and hips where Dev had held him still, and rubbed his thumbs lovingly over them. He decided to rent a house near a clifftop as soon as the residency had finished, where he could spend some solid time writing and where he could let the sea spray hollow him out and carry away his grief. He emailed his agent, and rang his parents to ask them if he could borrow the dog to take with him for company.

The place he chose overlooked the Pembrokeshire coastal path, and he took himself on long walks with his parents' Labrador, who seemed baffled by the unfamiliar landscape. Dev had only returned one in three of his messages since after the night of his birthday, and so one evening he went down to the beach and built a tiny burial mound out of slate around the napkin with Dev's number on it, planning to burn it, but at the last minute snatching it away.

He told himself he was an embarrassment, and went to coax the dog away from the pile of seaweed she sat hopefully in front of. He watched TV until his eyes hurt and went to bed with a bottle of whisky. He forced himself to remember the reasons they'd left each other, and these reasons had little hooks, and they joined up with and stuck to others and expanded to fill his thoughts, and by morning he felt as if he didn't miss Dev at all. Oh, his mind and bruised heart tried to catch him out, and he almost sent Dev a picture he'd taken of a particularly startling sunset, but he fought the impulse down. He went to Picton Castle and made pencil studies of the stones and moss, hoping someone would ask to see them, but they didn't. He did some modest climbing, and drove into the nearest town every morning to go to the swimming pool. The smell of chlorine that clung to him as he picked his way down the smuggler's path to the beach every day made him feel triumphant, as if he'd got something over on someone.

When he got back to London, he bumped into Dev and his new boyfriend walking on Kenwood on the first floral day of the year, and he made a show of shaking them both by the hand. The new boyfriend wore a complicated runner's watch, and he kept frowning down at it then up at the sky, occupied in some private and obscure ritual. When he'd finished and had gone off to get them all ice creams, Dev told Michael that he missed him, and he was only with Joe to keep his mind busy. 'I've changed, I'll change, it'll be different this time,' he said. It was spring and Michael shook his head mutely, furious at the way his treacherous heart bloomed at the words.

It was summer and Michael had deleted Dev's number and finished his book, and his editor had at last agreed to work on it with him. He won an international prize for a short story he'd written and forgotten about, and his phone began to ring again. He made an effort to go out on dates, even liking a few of the men he met, and whenever he saw friends he would say, 'This is one of me, moving on with my life.' They all pretended to believe him, and smiled discreetly at their drinks. Dev was promoted to senior curator, and let his finger hover over Michael's name and number for full seconds as he sent out invitations for the celebration, before moving past it.

It was summer and the heavy honey of the May days had been dishonest, because it rained all the time. When it wasn't raining, the days were warm and greyly clouded, so it was too hot to wear anything other than summer clothes. The lack of light made their fabric feel grubby and used-up, and Michael felt as if he had a belt tied tight around his ribs stopping him from properly filling his lungs. He was invited to a careers event at his old school to give a talk on what it was like to be a prize-winning author, and at the last minute decided to take the train instead of driving.

If he was going to be near his old school, he thought, he needed to be as close to his youthful mindset as possible, and to this end he rang his mother to ask her to pick him up from the station. Over wine which he was sure was the same that was always available at Dev's gallery events, he was approached by a man who he faintly recognised, who turned out to have been in his GCSE English class and was now a teacher there. He asked how Michael was these days, and how long he would be in town, and from the way his ears reddened Michael could tell that he'd discovered one or two things about himself since their schooldays. They made a plan to go for dinner the next evening, and when he told his mother that he would be out, her face fell briefly and she asked if he ever heard from Dev. The things he could say roiled up from his gut and burnt his mouth, but in the end he only shook his head.

Michael became obsessed with the idea that his flat would become flooded if it didn't stop raining, and he began to live nocturnally, shored up by a superstitious conviction that he could ward off the water through wakefulness. Flooding didn't happen during the day, he reasoned, as he opened up the endless list of copy-edits he was working through. He became pale and strange, and on the day the sun finally appeared he blinked against it as it warmed the wet paving-stones and made them smell once more of memory. He went out into a fresh rural-seeming morning, and went to the park where he trod water into his shoes.

Dev was also happy that the rain had stopped, and that Saturday went out for his first run since the spring. He found that elation and purpose filled his lungs and numbed out his legs, so by the time he'd returned he was glossy with sweat and breathing hard. He went back out to pick up the paper, and saw that the review section had a picture of Michael and three others he didn't recognise on the front alongside a story about the new crop of young British novelists. He took it home and pored over it, reading the words about Michael over and over again, and staring at the picture to see if any sense could be made of it. He kept the section even when it began to perfume the air with the smell of damp newsprint, and guarded it against his housemates, who itched to throw it away. He read it with purpose, as if by being industrious he would find new words and new thoughts that had appeared overnight, as if the print would unfurl and turn over revelations like fresh earth. He treated it like prayer, and practised every day, but the words stayed stubborn and fixed rigid. He threw the paper away.

It was summer and Michael couldn't sleep, because Michael missed a boy. The appearance of the sun had turned out to be another coy piece of dishonesty, and the rain was back in earnest. He sat on his window seat, with a duvet around his shoulders, and looked out balefully at the burnished patent-leather pavement, the street lights swimming in opaque orange haloes, like fireflies seen through thick glass. He'd finished his edits and was in limbo waiting for a response, and so could barely concentrate on anything apart from checking to see if it had arrived. A tiny window of attention had been left open in his mind for pulpy crime fiction, which he read by the fist-load and then forgot immediately, and he'd just read the last line of a satisfyingly hideous one when a boom of thunder shot up his spine and blossomed into goose pimples.

He brought his balled fist up under his chin, and dug his nails through the napkin he gripped there. The rain had been whispering, but now came down in roaring sheets. He opened up his fist, and looked down at the now indecipherable ink, and thought of the many ways that Dev had destroyed and then created him, and he thought of his demands and his ways and his intrusions, and the way he still couldn't peel a carrot, and that it didn't matter that he couldn't read the napkin, because the numbers still stood out in his mind like flame. He sat up straight and shrugged the duvet off, reaching for his phone before he could change his mind. Dev sounded bleary when he picked up, and Michael realised that it must be after two, but his words and feelings were a burst river bank and could not be blocked or derailed by apologies.

'Come back to me,' he said.

It was summer when on the other end of the phone Dev said yes.

Carys Bray is the author of a collection of short stories, *Sweet Home*, and two novels, *A Song for Issy Bradley*, which was shortlisted for the Costa Book Awards, and *The Museum of You*.

Rowan Hisayo Buchanan is the author of the novel *Harmless Like You*, and her short work has appeared in, among other places, the *Harvard Review*, *TriQuarterly*, and NPR's *Selected Shorts*.

Bernardine Evaristo is the award-winning author of seven books, including her most recent novel, *Mr Loverman* (Hamish Hamilton/Penguin-Random House, 2013).

Grace McCleen studied English Literature at Oxford and York Universities. She has written three critically acclaimed novels and reviews fiction for national newspapers.

Donal Ryan was born in Tipperary in 1976; he's a novelist, short-story writer and Fellow of the University of Limerick.

Nikesh Shukla is the author of *Coconut Unlimited*, *Meatspace* and *The Time Machine*, the editor of the collection *The Good Immigrant* and a sitcom writer.

D. W. Wilson is a short-story writer, novelist, Canadian citizen by birth and temperament, video game nerd, teacher, and redneck – among other things. He is currently between books, but his previous works are a short story collection, *Once You Break a Knuckle*, and *Ballistics*, a novel.

–

Phoebe Roy is a writer from London and the winner of the SceptreLoves short story prize.